The Widow in the Woods

The Widow in the Woods

Daisy Luther

Banned Books Publishing

Cheyenne, Wyoming

This is for my partners in crime – my daughters and my brilliant friends – who helped me create this book and perfect all sorts of imaginary mayhem. Thank you to all the people who helped me answer questions like, "how long would this take to kill someone?" and "how would you deal with this criminal if you were Grace?" without batting an eye.

My daughters

Chloe & Rachel

My friends

Brian, Cat, Chris, Chuck, Selco, Scott, Shaw, &Toby

I'm now quite certain we could plot and commit multiple murders together, then creatively get rid of the bodies, no problem.

Chapter 1

Not much had changed for Grace Sherwood.

Sure, she used candlelight, brought water in with a bucket, and heated with firewood now, but she'd often done that in the past. When she first moved to the old cottage in the mountains with her husband all those years ago when he returned from Vietnam, it took months before they were able to afford to hook up the power and water. They simply used the things that had been in place for the almost two centuries the small house had been standing. At the time, they were young and thought it was ridiculously romantic.

There was an outhouse set back from the house, and if outhouses could be adorable, this one was. It was a little stone outbuilding with the classic crescent moon carved into the faded, blue-painted door. A handpump stood in the mossy sideyard, and a few minutes of pumping brought forth fresh, sweet well water.

Inside the cozy cottage, there was the one thing that Grace had demanded: a wood stove with a flat top on which she could cook. The little home was made of stone, and James had said that it was so solid that it would probably be standing for a couple hundred years after they died. The cottage was like something from a fairy tale, and it blended in so well with the beautiful mountain setting that it almost appeared to have evolved naturally in the forest instead of being built there. A winding gravel path with one lane led you to the house if you knew it was there, but Grace had purposely allowed the entrance to the driveway to become obscured and overgrown when things began to go sideways.

For Grace, while things were not quite as easy as they were during The Before, she was still content in the home she had loved for more than 50 years.

Back when her television antenna could still pick up the news, she heard talk of a massive event that had rocked the United States, creating what Grace called The After. She didn't really pay much attention to the bigger details surrounding the disaster, so isolated was she in her little mountain home. She figured at least half of what the press reported was lies and the other half was spin. The news wasn't known for its honesty and credibility. It hadn't been since the days when Walter Cronkite had signed off with, "And that's the way it was." And sometimes Grace wondered if it had been even then.

Instead, she focused on the things that affected her directly – there was no more electrical service, no more phone service, and no more internet. She had enough propane to get her through a couple of years of judicious use, and she'd figure the rest out.

She had talked to her sons regularly until the phone lines went down. Jim, was a doctor in a rural part of Canada, and William was in Chicago, working in advertising, living in a high-rise.

They'd always been very close, but living hundreds to thousands of miles away in a crisis like the one happening now meant she might never see her boys again. She hoped that they remembered the lessons they'd learned on the little homestead where they grew up. She knew that wherever they were, they were helping others. It's how she had raised them, and Jim and Will had both become fine young men.

Grace missed them with her whole heart. She was sometimes lonely in her home in the forest.

From what she had seen, people in the cities were rioting, starving, and pleading for help. She felt sorry for them, especially the children who had no choice but to abide by the decisions of their parents, whether for better or for worse. She included her fervent good wishes for those involved each night as she lit candles in her little cottage to break the unrelenting darkness that blanketed the forest.

Grace hadn't been one for going into the city since she was young, back when her sense of adventure was far more acute. She had even lived in the Big Apple before it became rotten to the core with crime and violence. She'd had all kinds of excitement back in the day, but now, all she wanted was to tend her garden, do some needlepoint, and read some books. Being alone didn't really bother her anymore. She had lived by herself since her husband James had died ten years ago, and while she missed him desperately, she was otherwise content with the quiet life of plants, crafting, and reading books.

Since her telephone no longer worked, people didn't call her for help delivering babies or for herbal remedies anymore. Before the fall, she had delivered half the babies in the area and helped people with health matters, from itchy rashes to arthritis to far more serious issues.

Grace was something of a legend to the locals, an old-fashioned midwife and herbalist who stepped in when there were no modern doctors available.

But now, Grace was so far up the mountain and so hidden in the trees that it seemed as though the world had forgotten all about her. Nobody had shown up in months to the cheekily named home that she and James had called Sherwood Forest, an ode to the legend of Robin Hood. And from what Grace had seen before the television and power went out, that was probably for the best. Her home was so difficult to reach that it was as though the world had forgotten all about her.

Sometimes, she wondered if her life really had that much purpose anymore.

...

On this particular evening, the sky had been threatening, dark clouds seeming to boil in the dusky light. After she locked her chickens securely in their coop, Grace went inside and made herself a cup of tea using chamomile from her garden and sweetened with rich, thick forest honey from her hives. She kicked off her boots and settled into the handmade pillows cushioning the rocking chair on her front porch. She was all set to watch the storm.

Mother Nature was putting on quite a show before the rain began falling, with thunder rolling and lightning crackling across the sky. "Better than anything on television," Grace said to her one companion, her cat, Nightshade. He was a dark gray feline that she had found as a kitten. He'd somehow gotten into the part of the garden that she kept fenced off behind a sturdy locked gate that was meant to protect animals with two legs and four from the plants within. The scraggly little kitten had been just fine in there with the plants that could cure or kill, depending on the dose, which was why she opted to name him after one of them.

The clouds burst open, and the downpour began. The sound of the rain pounding the porch's tin roof almost drowned out the sound of the thunder. Lightning illuminated her gardens and the trees beyond them to a brief brightness that rivaled a moment of daylight.

And it was the lightning that showed her *someone* – she had no idea who – was out there in the forest surrounding her home.

Grace wasn't afraid, per se, but she was unsettled. It had been months since she'd seen anybody, and she was concerned that it was a person up to no good. Perhaps it was someone from the city who had made the long journey out to her little wooded oasis in search of food and shelter. That could go either way – hunger caused a kind of existential desperation that made nearly any person untrustworthy.

Grace studiously looked away from where she had seen the person and sipped her tea. She discreetly patted the pocket of her voluminous apron to reassure herself that her ever-present Glock was indeed nestled in her pocket. She was a skilled seamstress and had sewn a little holster into the pockets of all her aprons to keep her firearm secure. She was generally a good neighbor to the animals of the forest, but living out here alone, it was only common sense to be armed, just in case one of the creatures chose to violate their unspoken peace treaty.

The next flash of lightning illuminated a young girl who appeared in front of her steps as if by magic. The thin girl was soaked to the skin and shivering in the rain in her t-shirt and jeans. Her face was pale, and her dark hair was plastered to it. Her big brown eyes were wide with fright. Grace assumed she was afraid of the storm, and her heart melted.

That was Grace's first mistake.

"Hello," she greeted the girl warmly. "Would you like to come in out of the rain?"

The girl's eyes widened even more if such a thing was possible, and she froze in place, getting pelted by the rain. She looked like she'd been turned to stone.

Grace padded down the three steps in her bare feet. "Come on, my girl, let's get you dried off and warm."

The girl began to shake her head frantically in silent warning.

"We'd love to get warm," said a male voice.

Grace suddenly found herself outnumbered. She willed herself not to touch the gun in her pocket and give away her advantage. Two men and a woman joined the girl. "I'm Christopher, and this is Beth and my brother Luke," he introduced himself and gestured toward the two adults. "The girl is Lexie."

The man who spoke was tall and very good-looking. He smiled at Grace wryly in an attempt to be disarming, but she had always been a woman of quick discernment. And she did not like this man, not one bit. She noted that the girl had begun to tremble even harder when she was joined by the trio, and she suspected that she'd been wrong in her assessment: her fear had nothing to do with the storm.

The man whistled sharply, and two more men appeared at the yard's edge, one supporting the other. The woman quickly joined them to help, and Grace could see that the one being supported was younger, perhaps in his late teens, and his shirt was soaked in blood.

She couldn't fight all of them. She knew she had no option but to play along and let them into her haven if she wanted to stay alive. She'd get her chance later.

"Come in," she said with a cordiality that belied her instant mistrust. "I have some medical training. I can help your friend.

Chapter 2

Hunger is a powerful motivator, but fear is more powerful still. When bad things happen to you, sometimes all you can do is play along and try not to make things worse. Sometimes, you have to retreat into the only safe place you have: silence.

Lexie White was 15 years old, and she hadn't said a word in six months. Her voice was the only thing she could control, and the only stubborn streak of rebellion she had left was her refusal to speak.

Things had gone bad when the country began to devolve into chaos caused by a complete breakdown of the way things were. She didn't completely understand what had caused things to go upside-down, but she knew that there were no longer food deliveries made because there was no food to be had. If you didn't already possess supplies, you were out of luck.

Lexie's family was fortunate in that they had been preparing for a long time. Her parents were well prepped for almost any scenario.

The unfortunate part came later when the neighbors discovered that they had supplies. That was the one scenario her parents were not ready for.

Her father, the kindest man she'd ever known, had always disliked the Hill brothers. That was saying a lot because he found the good in everyone. He wouldn't allow Lexie to be outside when they were out in the driveway, swigging beer and working on cars. He told her that they weren't trustworthy and that it wasn't safe for her to be around them. She remembered how she had rolled her eyes affectionately at what she thought was overprotectiveness.

Despite his dislike of the neighbors, when they came to him for help a few months after things had gone sideways, he offered them a hot meal and some supplies.

And that was when everything had gone horribly wrong.

Christopher Hill, the oldest brother, had not been satisfied with the generous gift. Oh, he had pretended and acted ingratiatingly grateful, but suddenly Lexie saw the meanness behind his handsome smile. She saw exactly what her father had been talking about, and realized that he'd been right.

Lots of women had tried to capture the heart of the good-looking man with dark hair and vivid blue eyes. But before, when there were laws and cops, he couldn't get away with being who he was deep down inside. He wasn't in it for love and romance. He wanted power and control. He wanted victims. He wanted to indulge in things that would have once gotten him locked up.

She told her mother she was uncomfortable with how Christopher looked at her, how he made her skin crawl by staring just a little too long. But she was just a girl, and her parents were fine people who couldn't imagine how dark people could really be. While they had never liked the Hills, they thought it was her imagination, an exaggeration of her bookworm brain and vivid imagination.

It wasn't.

One night, about a week after her father had generously handed over supplies, they came back.

Christopher and his brothers, Luke, Rick, and Jon, had killed her family with sadistic glee. She watched the whole thing, unable to flee or hide because Luke's girlfriend held her in place, making her an unwilling witness. Beth had laughed at Lexie's anguish when her parents were murdered right in front of her eyes.

Lexie wished fervently that they had killed her, too, because the things that Christopher made her do were worse than death.

The Hill brothers got increasingly plainer, like a printer that had less ink with each copy, creating a more dim likeness each time. Jon, the youngest brother, was the plainest of all. His hair was merely brown, not a swoop of raven. His eyes were so pale blue that they seemed faded. He wasn't quite as overtly brutal as the others. Lexie figured that maybe the meanness faded right along with the looks.

They carelessly went through the supplies that Mr. White had carefully stored in no time at all, wasting valuable resources, and then they all left in the family's van, dragging Lexie screaming and crying with them until they could no longer siphon gas out of other abandoned vehicles. Then, they set off on foot in search of other people with food and water. They were like a horde of locusts, except locusts merely acted on instinct to eat. The Hills enjoyed the pain and fear they inflicted on their victims.

Luke's girlfriend, Beth, despised Lexie and treated her like a slave. She woke most mornings to a sharp kick to her ribs from Beth's pointed boot, only to spend the day walking, cooking, gathering wood, and carrying water. Beth was lovely, if you overlooked the cruelty in her narrowed eyes. She had vivid red hair, pale, flawless skin, and a perfect smile. But if you looked into her eyes, you could see the darkness there, in the green depths.

After a month, Lexie had cried so much that no more tears would come. It was like she'd only been allotted a certain number of tears for her lifetime, and she'd sobbed all of them out during her first four weeks In Hell. That was her calendar, her measuring point. Before Hell and In Hell.

The only rebellion she had left was refusing to speak. It irked Christopher, causing him to do upsetting things just to try and make her beg him to stop. She quickly learned not to let her emotions show on her face, extending her silence to her expression. It enraged Beth, who was Luke's girlfriend, but inexplicably strove to impress Christopher. Beth regularly pinched and kicked Lexie, hoping to illicit a shriek from the girl.

It was Lexie's sixth month In Hell when they picked the wrong farmhouse to attack. They always forced her to go to the door first, by herself, acting like she needed help. She refused to speak to the homeowners, too, and hated her part in this. Without fail, people felt sorry for the pale, thin girl and wanted to help her.

When they opened the door, the Hill brothers and Beth rushed the homeowners, killing the men. Sometimes they raped the women, sometimes they killed them because they put up too much of a fight. Lexie regularly regretted that she had not put up more of a battle, so they'd have killed her, too.

They were making their way up the narrow mountain road, using up supplies at one home, then moving on to the next cabin. All the houses here were isolated, which meant that people had let their guards down. It also meant nobody could hear the screaming as the families were brutally attacked. Nobody could help.

But the last house had defenses that the brothers had not expected. There were a couple of hidden family members who were guarding the house. The gang came under heavy fire when they tried to push their way in. Rick had taken a bullet to the side, and there was no choice but to retreat. Lexie resisted then. She scratched and clawed and kicked, struggling to get away. She wanted to stay with the family who had successfully fought off the Hill brothers. The last thing she remembered was a sharp pain in her jaw and then there was nothing but darkness.

...

When Lexie came to, her jaw hurt so much she wasn't sure if she could eat. Christopher had punched her and thrown her over his shoulder as they fled. He wasn't willing to lose his prize.

Rick was asleep on the ground beside her, blood soaking his formerly gray tee shirt. A makeshift bandage had been created from an extra shirt, wrapped around his torso but doing little to stop the seeping from the wound. She knew from the first aid class she'd taken to be a babysitter that direct pressure was needed to stop the bleeding, but she wasn't about to volunteer that information. If he died, that was one less Hill brother to make her life miserable.

Jon returned to the camp, jubilant. "I found us another place, and it's just an old lady. There's food and a garden and chickens," he informed them, filled with self-importance. "We could stay there a long time."

Lexie quietly made her way around the camp, gathering fallen sticks for the fire. She didn't talk, but she certainly listened. She willed herself to be invisible, wishing many times each day that she actually possessed the magical power to disappear. She got as close to invisibility as possible, averting her gaze, refusing to speak, and making as little noise as possible as she went about her daily tasks.

The plan was to wait until it was dark, then send Lexie to the door yet again. She wished she could help the people that they were raiding. But she had no options whatsoever. Any fight she put up would lead to unspeakable things, things so depraved she never in her wildest nightmares could have thought such acts existed. She had realized after just a few days with Christopher that the devil was not an ugly, horned creature. He was a tall, dark-haired, handsome man with twinkling blue eyes and dimples encircling a charming smile.

As night began to fall, the sky began to roil with clouds. Thunder and lightning created an atmosphere as spooky as any book Lexie had ever read.

And when she approached the front porch silently in the rain, she realized that if demons existed in human form, perhaps angels did too.

The lady sitting on her rocking chair held a cup that sparkled in the flickering light. She had long silver braids that gleamed when lightning danced across the sky. If it weren't for the color of her hair, she could have been any age. Her tan skin appeared unlined, and her long, flowy dress stopped just above her ankles and bare feet when she stood. Lexie could see kindness in her the same way she saw meanness in the Hills and Beth. Her cat, startled, vanished off the porch into the forest in a streak of gray.

She stopped short of the porch, trying to wordlessly convey with her eyes that the lovely older woman was in danger. She couldn't make herself take another step if it meant putting that woman in danger. She shook her head frantically to warn her, but it was too late. The lady didn't understand the message Lexie was trying to get across.

Christopher stepped up beside her, that sickeningly charming smile pasted on his face. He put his arm loosely over Lexie's shoulders, and she forced herself not to flinch away. Her face became a mask once again, expressionless and numb.

Then, in a moment of communication that felt almost telepathic, she realized that the beautiful old woman saw everything with clarity, too. It filled her with a wild burst of hope, quickly followed by dread. She had seen the Hills in action.

What chance could an old lady possibly stand against that kind of evil? Even if that old lady was an angel in human form?

Chapter 3

"Come in," Grace extended the invitation warmly. "I have medical training. I can help your friend."

"He's my baby brother," the tall, dark-haired man said with a beautiful, warm smile. "I'd be very grateful for your help. Family means everything to me."

Grace wasn't fooled by his charm and good looks. There were some people who just emanated evil. Even if she hadn't seen the cruelty within him, she would have known by how the pale girl somehow became even paler. Grace had never had a daughter, only sons, who were now long lost to her from the event that had changed the world, but she could see that horrible damage had been inflicted on this child by the man who casually showed his ownership with his arm draped over her slender shoulders.

He said all the right words, had all the right facial expressions and intonations, but Grace's sharp instincts prevented her from being taken in. He was a wolf in an incredibly handsome sheep costume, and she knew it.

She turned and opened the screen door, allowing the invaders into her home. "Will you walk into my parlor?" she quoted the old poem, hoping that the girl was a reader. Someone was going to be the spider, and someone was going to be the fly. Who was who would soon be determined.

As they helped the wounded man up the steps, Grace opened her hall closet and pulled out a plastic sheet. She rapidly spread it across the daybed in her front room and gestured for them to put him there.

Grace returned to the closet and grabbed her worn leather medical bag. She hadn't used it much recently, but the tools within felt as familiar to her hands as her garden tools did. She had delivered many babies, both the human type and fur-covered livestock, using the tools in that bag. She'd also performed a number of other procedures and stitched up more than one wound in her day.

She showed the men her scissors before cutting off the wounded man's shirt. He was barely conscious. "What's your name, young man?" she asked, peering at the bullet hole in his upper abdomen.

"Rick Hill," he gasped, groaning in pain.

"Well, Rick Hill, I'm going to have to get this bullet out of you, but you're going to be okay," Grace informed him briskly. She turned to the others. "I have to go out to my greenhouse and get some supplies."

"What kind of supplies?" demanded Beth suspiciously.

"Some herbs to help his pain and some to prevent infection."

"Go with her, Jon," Christopher ordered. The youngest man of the group stood up and joined Grace.

"Wonderful. You can help me carry things," Grace said, as though the entire thing was her idea.

Wordlessly, she picked up a flashlight and went out the back door. She strode across the brick pavers to the little greenhouse where she grew medicinal herbs year-round and concocted her mixtures. The greenhouse was complete with a tiny, efficient woodstove where she could boil water, melt beeswax, and sterilize supplies.

Grace didn't just make medicines here, however. This greenhouse was also her workshop. She had spent many hours there, dipping candles, slicing into cured homemade soap to turn it into fragrant bars, creating remedies, and concocting mixtures that made her garden thrive and pests flee.

Even with the gun in her pocket, Grace knew she didn't dare risk using it right away. No, she'd have to handle this slowly and meticulously, one by one. She might not be able to fight them and win in hand-to-hand combat, but she knew that in a battle of wits, she was far better armed than this evil group of people. Her husband had taught her that strategy was just as deadly a weapon as any firearm, given enough time to enact it.

As Jon watched her carefully, she picked up a large mason jar filled with a light brown liquid labeled "garden tea" and a vial on which she had handwritten "laudanum." Her laudanum was made from the opium poppies she'd grown from seeds her husband had brought to her when he returned from Vietnam. She had a thriving patch of poppies that burst into glorious red flame every year. She added some cinnamon and cloves she had stored and some saffron threads from her patch of purple flowers, mashed it all up, and soaked it in alcohol.

Then, she decanted the mixture into vials each year for the treatment of pain or relentless diarrhea.

Her mission complete, she handed the jar to her escort, and they returned to the house.

Grace went straight to the kitchen, where she set a kettle on the stove and turned on the propane. She had carefully rationed it out and only turned it on when needed. Taking the extra step of having to turn it on and off reminded her to think about whether or not it was necessary. She had a couple of large tanks that she had fortunately filled right before things went sideways, and she figured she had enough to last at least another year if she used it sparingly. She took crisp, clean towels from the drawer, got a bowl, and mixed a few spoons full of the laudanum with honey from her hives. It would still taste awful – that was the nature of laudanum – but it would help to relieve the pain.

She added mint to two shiny silver-colored tea balls and poured the boiling water over them into two lovely china mugs embellished with delicate, hand-painted yellow flowers. She dribbled in some honey and left them on the counter to steep.

Next, she took the jar of dried parsley from her garden and stirred a handful into the jar marked "garden tea." Garden tea was the homemade fertilizer that she created when cleaning up after her hens. While the manure was too hot to put on her garden immediately, she could add some of it to water, let it sit for a while, then strain it out. She put the manure she strained out on her compost pile, and the strained liquid made an incredibly fertile addition to her tomato bed.

But it could serve another purpose. The garden tea would also serve to infect a wound she was claiming to treat.

One by one.

The parsley would help clot the blood and mask the smell of the tea somewhat, although with the solids drained out, the smell wasn't terribly strong and certainly wasn't obvious. She topped a basin with some cheesecloth and strained the garden tea while she gathered more supplies: a wooden spoon, a large syringe with a bulb, and the kettle as she returned to her patient. She handed the basin to Jon and together, they took everything to the parlor and sat it down on a marble-topped table beside the day bed. She went back to her medical closet and grabbed a fresh pile of gauze and bandages.

"Okay, Rick, I'm going to give you something for the pain," she announced.

"Wait," interrupted Beth suspiciously. "How do we know you aren't poisoning him?"

"Well, I suppose you don't. But I can give some to the young girl, too, as it appears she must have fallen into something and hurt her jaw," Grace smiled. It was a false smile that didn't really reach her eyes. Yeah, the girl had fallen into someone's fist. "You can watch her and then decide."

Christopher nodded. "Give Lexie the drug first."

Grace wiggled her finger to summon the girl to her. Lexie was a pale, pretty, haunted child. "I must warn you, dear, this tastes terrible. But it will help your jaw." It would also help her to sleep deeply and keep her away from the odious man in charge, at least for one night, Grace thought with satisfaction.

Lexie nodded and held the spoon while Grace poured the mixture of honey and laudanum into it. "I know it's bitter, but try to hold it under your tongue. It will work faster, and I have peppermint tea brewing to take the taste out of your mouth."

Lexie made a face at the horrible flavor of the laudanum. There wasn't enough honey in the world to make it palatable. But she didn't say a word, and she obediently held it under her tongue as Grace had directed.

The room was quiet as everyone watched Lexie. When she finally swallowed the laudanum, Grace said, "Now go get yourself a mug of tea from the kitchen and bring in the other one for Rick."

Lexie disappeared into the kitchen to do as Grace had instructed. When she returned, she sat stiffly on the edge of a plush violet-colored armchair on the other side of the room. It didn't take long until the laudanum began working magic, and she curled up in the big chair. She sipped her tea and pulled a soft, fuzzy blanket off the back of the chair to cover up. It had been knitted with yarn containing all the green shades of the forest. She was still damp from the rain, but she felt cozy and comfortable for the first time since she had been In Hell.

Rick moaned in pain.

"Go ahead," Christopher ordered. "Give him the medicine."

...

Christopher Hill wasn't accustomed to having things happen that were outside his control. Since he was a small boy, he'd been able to easily get his own way with a wink and an adorable smile. His mama had been wrapped around his pudgy little finger from the moment he was born, and things had only gotten better for him as he got older.

He realized when he was in sixth grade that he really wasn't like the other kids. They seemed to feel empathy, or at the very least, sympathy, when one of their classmates was in pain. Young Christopher had found it fascinating and it gave him a weird, good feeling to watch someone suffer.

By eighth grade, he realized it was even more fun for him if someone was suffering emotionally. His mama believed he was just a heartbreaker but Christopher knew it went deeper than that. He liked to pretend he was into a girl just so he could see how far he could manipulate her. Then he liked to leave her shattered and yearning for him while he moved on to his next victim.

By the time he graduated from high school, he was good -looking, suave, and charming. He worked in construction which gave him a strong, fit body, and he was soon visiting bars while he was underage and romancing women 5-10 years older than him, playing the same games he had in high school.

It had been a rush.

He knew that he was not a nice person. He didn't care one bit. In fact, he enjoyed it. Nice people finished last.

He had a few brushes with the law and spent a couple of nights in the county jail. That's when he knew he absolutely did not want to go to prison. He couldn't stand being in environments where he was not in control.

The only people he cared about on this earth were his mama and his younger brothers. He led his brothers through all types of mischief and helped them evade the law, providing what he believed to be a stabilizing influence since their drunk father had only been around enough to keep getting his mama knocked up.

When things had gone sideways, he had his first experience with grief. Mama had been sick, and suddenly, there was no medical help to be had. The pharmacies were closed, the hospital was closed, and there were no doctors available. He had broken into a pharmacy to steal some drugs for Mama, but he hadn't really known what to look for. Many of the supplies had already been picked over, probably by employees before they fled.

All his efforts had been in vain, and Mama died.

His heart was broken. He'd truly loved her, and she'd probably been the only female he'd ever adored and respected. Before she passed, she had gripped his arm with shocking strength in her frail hands. She had one request of her favorite son.

"You take care of your little brothers, do you hear me?"

"Yes, Mama." It had been hard to get the words out through the knot in his throat.

"Promise me. Swear it."

"I swear, Mama."

And then she was gone, leaving Christopher Hill in charge of Luke, Jon, and young Ricky.

And now, because of Christopher's actions, Rick was in peril.

He'd do whatever was necessary to ensure his brother survived.

...

"Don't spit this out. You need to hold it under your tongue. I have to remove the bullet, and this will help you withstand the pain," Grace told Rick firmly.

He nodded, and she spooned the bitter liquid into his mouth. He coughed a little but held it under his tongue. Grace spoon-fed him a few sips from the mug of tea to cleanse his mouth of the dreadful taste.

She sat in a chair beside him, picked up her needlepoint, put on her reading glasses, and began stitching. "What the hell are you doing?" barked Luke.

Grace peered sternly over her glasses, giving not an inch. "I'm giving the medicine time to work unless you'd prefer that I go digging for that bullet without pain relief."

Luke subsided sullenly and disappeared from the room. Grace heard noises from her kitchen that sounded like Luke was helping himself to a snack. Beth left the room to join him, followed by Jon, and soon, the room was filled with the smell of something delicious heating up on the stove. They'd found the chili she had pressure canned just last winter. Beth brought a bowl and spoon to Christopher. Lexie was sound asleep on the chair, not that Beth would have bothered bringing food for the girl. For a few minutes, the only sound was the clinking of spoons against pottery as the interlopers enjoyed her food.

Rick seemed to be getting some relief from the laudanum. Jon, Luke, and Beth had returned from the kitchen. It was time.

"I'm going to need some help from you young men," Grace informed them. "I need you to hold your brother down while I get this bullet out."

Jon and Luke took their stations at Rick's shoulders and feet. Grace had seen bullet wounds before, and she was nearly certain this one hadn't hit anything terribly important. But the bullet had to come out. And even if the wound wasn't lethal now, it would be by the time she was finished.

She used the lit candle in the cozy little parlor to sterilize the long, stainless steel medical tweezers, then poured a little of the laudanum mixture over them to cool them down. She lifted Rick's shirt and nodded to Jon and Luke. "You mustn't let him move, or this will do more harm than good."

They pinned him down firmly. Grace placed the wooden spoon in between his teeth.

She inserted the tweezers as gently as she could, feeling around with them to get a sense of the angle of the wound. She followed it carefully and felt it when the instrument touched the metal of the bullet. Rick was screaming around the spoon and would have been thrashing on the sofa to escape the prodding if his brothers hadn't been holding him so firmly. Finally, mercifully, he went still as it became too much for him, and he lost consciousness. Grace was relieved, as she hated inflicting pain. Victoriously, she pulled out the bullet and dropped it into the mug of tea with a plop.

She turned to the basin containing the garden tea and parsley mixture she had strained. Using a large syringe that looked suspiciously like a Thanksgiving turkey baster, she began to irrigate the wound with the tainted liquid. After several minutes of the treatment, the blood coming out of the wound ran pink. Grace topped the area with a stack of folded gauze and added direct pressure. When it appeared that the bleeding had slowed, she taped the bandage into place.

Grace returned to the kitchen and dumped the liquid from the basin back into the jar from whence it came. She put the lid on the jar of garden tea tightly. She'd be using that concoction daily to "clean" Rick's wound. She washed her hands in the kitchen basin using her home-made soap, then washed the dishes that Jon, Luke, and Beth had left carelessly on the counter.

She returned to the parlor, the perfect hostess. "Would you like me to show you to your beds?" It appeared that Beth and Luke had helped themselves to some of the laudanum in her absence. They were slurring their words when they talked, giggling softly and nodding off on the sofa.

She led them upstairs and directed the couple to the upstairs guest room. Jon was given the pullout sofa in her sewing room. She gave Christopher the master bedroom. Grace had already pegged him as the type of person who wanted to be venerated and feared. It would work to her advantage if she treated him like the king he thought he was and bided her time. *His arrogance*, she mused, *will give me the opening I need and be the end of him.*

She returned to the parlor and checked on her patient. Rick was asleep, pale, and still on the daybed. She touched his forehead, checking for fever. He was cool. *For now*, she thought.

Then Grace turned to the big chair where the girl was curled up, sound asleep. She pulled the blanket up over Lexie's slender shoulders. She gently smoothed the girl's hair back from her face, examining the bruise on her jaw with disgust. She couldn't do much for her, but at least she could spare her one night of abuse.

Grace sunk down on the fluffy, overstuffed sofa and pulled over herself a heavy, handmade afghan dotted with crocheted roses. She never imagined she'd be able to sleep with everything that was going on, but somehow, she dropped off almost immediately.

Chapter 4

When Lexie woke up the next morning, she thought for a moment she was home. It felt like she was back in her bed, under the brightly colored quilt she'd had ever since she could remember. That quilt had become soft, almost satin-like, because of being washed so many times over the years. Before she opened her eyes, Lexie nestled deeper under the covers and touched the familiar hem of the quilt...

And then she awakened fully, with a devastating mental jolt that felt like a shock of electricity.

She was not home.

It hadn't all been a horrific nightmare.

She looked around the room through slitted eyes, pretending to still be sleeping. She was on a soft, plump overstuffed chair, the kind that had room for two if you wanted to cuddle. The crisp fabric of a pillowcase was cool under her cheek. The room smelled of herbs, beeswax, and old books. She could dimly see through her lashes. There was furniture in shades of warm red, rich green, and lush purple, surrounded by darkly gleaming wood walls. A lacy curtain fluttered in a gentle breeze, filtering the morning sunlight into the room. While it wasn't the bedroom she had dreamed she was in, it was cozy and comforting.

Lexie wanted to pretend to be asleep and stay in that chair forever, but she desperately needed to relieve her bladder. She finally, grudgingly, couldn't wait anymore. She sat up and her feet had just touched the floor when the voice of the angel startled her.

"Good morning, sweetheart – do you need to go outside?" Grace whispered. "You fell asleep before I could show you where the outhouse was."

Lexie nodded, and the woman gave her a "come this way" gesture. She eyed Rick suspiciously, giving the daybed where he slept a wide berth.

They both padded, barefoot, to the back door where some large, broken-down boots awaited their feet. The screen door squeaked as Grace pushed it open, and she led Lexie down a path to an adorable little building with a faded blue door. Lexie went first, enjoying the privacy of the four walls after being accustomed to surreptitiously squatting outdoors.

When they were both finished, Grace said softly, "I'm going to make breakfast for everyone. Would you help me?"

Lexie nodded and followed Grace to the coziest kitchen imaginable. There was both an old-fashioned wood burning kitchen stove and a small gas range attached to a propane tank. The walls were a buttery yellow, and the cupboards were a gleaming warm-toned wood that were so polished Lexie was sure that if she looked hard, she would see the light dusting of freckles on her nose reflected back to her.

Grace got an onion and some potatoes from the wooden cupboard with mesh doors and plucked some herbs from the sunny window adorned with another lace curtain. She put a knife and a cutting board down on the counter and showed Lexie how she wanted the potatoes cut. Eggs from a bowl on the counter were broken into a cheerful red floral bowl and whipped with a hand beater. Grace added some lard to a frying pan and turned on the precious gas to heat it up.

Lexie held the knife in her hand after the vegetables were chopped. She didn't want to relinquish it and did so grudgingly when Grace gently took it from her. "Now isn't the time, sweet girl," she murmured.

Lexie released the knife into Grace's custody and felt bereft.

Grace dished up breakfast for the visitors. She made each plate lovely, sprinkling the eggs with some of the dried Parmesan cheese powder from a canister. Se used a dainty spoon to sprinkle another white powder onto only two servings of eggs.

Then she added a flourish of green dried parsley from a jar and a generous grind of black pepper to each plate.

The unwelcome visitors had begun to stir as the smell of onions and potatoes frying drifted up the stairs. Grace brought water to boil on another burner and added it to the French press, where she had her own mixture of a few coffee beans and some roasted chicory root from her garden. She sprinkled in a little cinnamon and briskly took an amber bottle off the shelf. The bottle was equipped with a dropper and the white-haired woman added a generous amount to the press.

When Lexie tilted her head to the side curiously, Grace told her, "This is chasteberry. It grows on that pretty purple bush outside and I began to grow it when I took care of women's health. It has many other purposes, too, and tastes sort of like black pepper." She left the French press on the counter to brew her concoction. Unbeknownst to Lexie, one of the other uses of chasteberry was to cool men's desires. It had been used in the Middle Ages by monks to help them maintain their vows of purity, and Grace hoped it would lessen Christopher's interest in Lexie.

Lexie nodded and pulled down enough charmingly mismatched china cups for everyone and put them on the counter beside the French press. She watched solemnly from the furthest corner of the kitchen she could squeeze into as Beth and the brothers trickled into the kitchen.

Ever inconsiderate, they drained the French press without leaving any coffee behind. Grace quietly set another kettle full of water on to boil for some tea for herself and Lexie.

"Be careful," she warned with a smile. "This breakfast is very rich and could upset your stomach if you aren't accustomed to eating like this."

Christopher laughed, and the rest of them flatly ignored her, cleaning their plates in record time.

Grace handed Lexie one of the plates that had the white powder on it. She tasted it suspiciously and it seemed fine. She wondered what it was, but not enough to stop eating. If someone had assured her the white powder was rat poison that would cause her rapid and untimely death, she still would have eaten the delicious food. The eggs were so fluffy and the potatoes so crisp that she marveled at how such tasty and decadent food was still available in the devolving world. Lexie silently devoured every bite with the hunger of a person who hadn't had a good meal in a long time. Grace stood beside her at the counter, nibbling at the food on her own plate. Her plate, Lexie had noticed, was *not* one of the ones with the white powder. She wasn't sure who'd gotten the other one, but her stomach was comfortably full for the first time in ages, and she didn't give it more thought.

"Let's go get some water for washing up," she told Lexie, pointing to a bucket in the sink.

"Wait," Christopher interrupted. "Where do you think you're taking her?"

"Just to carry a bucket of water," Grace assured him. "You'll be able to see us from the window without even leaving your chair."

She paused, awaiting his permission. He nodded abruptly.

They went out to the side yard where an old red hand pump stood. Grace showed her how to pump the water, and Lexie carried the heavy, sloshing vessel back inside.

"You can wash the dishes, Lexie, my girl," Grace instructed as she grabbed her medical kit to go care for the patient in the living room.

Lexie plugged the sink and added a bit of the soap from the container on the counter. Wordlessly, she cleared the empty plates from the table as Beth and the brothers sat there, expecting to be waited on. She flinched reflexively when Christopher shoved his wooden chair back with a startling squeeaaak across the linoleum floor. Beth snickered mockingly at Lexie's response, but for once, Christopher wasn't paying attention to the young girl. Instead, he was following Grace into the parlor where his injured brother lay.

Chapter 5

Rick remained asleep on the daybed, as still as the dead. His pale cheeks all but blended into the white pillowcase beneath his head. When Grace touched him, his skin was clammy. He peered at her groggily as she pulled down the sheets to check his wound.

The wound looked less angry than it had when she had removed the bullet. Grace clucked her tongue and wordlessly got up to get her special wound dressing and supplies from the kitchen.

As she walked to the kitchen to fetch the jar of garden tea and some laudanum, she felt closer to James than she had in a very long time. She could almost hear his voice, telling her stories of the Viet Cong and how they ensured that anyone who was wounded by one of their punji sticks would succumb to infection. She wished that it worked faster. She could almost hear his warm chuckle as he teased her about her lack of patience.

Tears filled her eyes for just a quick, blinding second, but she blinked them back. She had no time for sentimental nonsense right now.

Lexie sat stiffly at the kitchen table, alone. Grace gave her a wink and gathered her supplies. "Do you know how to weed a vegetable garden, my girl?" she questioned.

Lexie nodded wordlessly. Grace opened a drawer and handed her a pair of worn gloves with a faded pink floral pattern. "Go out and do so, please, dear. You'll be safe there. Don't go into the area with the wall around it." The screen door squeaked as Lexie left the kitchen.

After a couple of months with the group, Christopher no longer felt it necessary to guard Lexie every second of the day. He was supremely confident that he had broken her spirit and that she'd never dare to betray her or try to escape.

Grace gathered her jar of garden tea and the syringe and added laudanum and honey to a cup. While she fully intended that Rick's wound be fatal, she wouldn't inflict pointless suffering on any living creature. The laudanum would help him through the pain of the sepsis she intended to induce. She stopped in the hallway to grab more fresh gauze.

Grace returned to the kitchen to get the mug, then handed the cup of painkiller to Christopher. "Give this to your brother before I begin cleaning his wound," she ordered. Christopher didn't look delighted to be taking orders, but he helped Rick sit up nonetheless and guided the cup to his mouth, whispering encouragement to his brother.

Once the laudanum had time to take effect, Grace began to work on the wound. What nourished the soil would do the opposite to a wound, she was most certain. She also knew that continuously flushing out a wound would prevent it from healing, which would give the bacteria she was introducing more time to work. Meanwhile, it looked to the untrained eye like Grace was diligently caring for a wounded man and doing her best to make him better.

As they left Rick fitfully resting, she pulled Christopher aside. "I'm worried about your brother. His wound doesn't look quite right to me."

Christopher flashed a beautiful smile. His straight white teeth and dimples belonged to a different man, a kind, charming man. It was like a disguise that hid the relentless rot of who he really was. But one thing about times like this one was that masks that worked in The Before began to slip and expose who people really were.

At least they did if you looked hard enough.

Unfortunately for her unwelcome guests, they weren't people who looked hard enough. When they looked at Grace, they only saw a sweet little old lady. They completely missed the streak of iron inside her, underneath her own mask.

It was that determination which had caused James to fondly nickname her "The General." He would say, "Whatever the General wants, the General will get" whenever some injustice made her angry.

He'd always had complete faith in her.

She hoped that his faith was not misplaced because two lives depended on her skills and her willingness to do whatever she had to do. She pulled her attention back to the handsome man in front of her.

"You don't know my brother," he stated with great confidence. "Hills don't die easy."

"It's a severe wound, and I just want you to be prepared – he has a rough road ahead of him," Grace warned.

Christopher chuckled dismissively and sat in the chair beside his brother. *He is very condescending*, thought Grace in silent satisfaction. *This will work against him because he thinks he's smarter than everyone else.*

He thinks he's smarter than me.

He'll never see it coming.

As she walked through the hallway, she stopped to peer at a sampler on the wall she had stitched herself. The sight of the carefully embroidered herbs, vines, leaves, bees, and flowers in it never failed to make her feel calm and centered. She counted the flowers and plants for a moment, then headed out to the garden.

She had some herbs to harvest.

...

Jon, Luke, and Beth were on the front porch, playing cards. Jon was relieved that he could pass the time this way. He really didn't enjoy the looting and killing the way Luke and Christopher did, but he understood the necessity of it.

It was "us" or "them" in the world right now. And Jon wasn't going to let his dislike of blood, guts, and tears get in the way of his survival.

If he'd had his way, he would hang back with Ricky while the others wrought havoc on the homes they visited. But, as Christopher insisted, they were a team and they had to all work together if they were going to survive.

It wasn't that Jon had high moral standards. He didn't care about the victims they left in their wake. He didn't like listening to screaming. He would rather come in once they were already dead so he didn't have to see the beseeching looks they cast his way, looking for help that would not come.

Because of his distaste for violence, it seemed like Jon was the nicest of the Hill brothers.

He was not.

He just didn't like getting his hands dirty.

He peered at Beth over his hand of cards. She was the most beautiful woman Jon had ever seen in his life, and if she hadn't been his brother's girl, he would have stopped at nothing to win her heart. But Beth was different than him. She had a wide streak of chaos in her that made her a perfect match for his wild brother, Luke. Together, they gloried in the fright of the families they were raiding. They thoroughly enjoyed the violence and the fear they instilled.

But Beth was still Beth.

Jon loved her. But he'd never make a move on her. He would always love his brothers more than anyone on this earth.

Chapter 6

Lexie wasn't feeling right. Her stomach was cramping, and she'd spent more time in the outhouse than she had in the garden. It appeared that she and Luke were taking turns in there because every time she wanted to go in, she saw him come out, pale and sweaty.

She wondered what that powder was Grace had put on her food. Had Grace *poisoned* her? Lexie was devastated. She thought that sweet little old lady was going to help her, but now she was feeling violently ill.

Nobody can be trusted, she raged inwardly. Her eyes darkened as they filled up with tears that threatened to spill down her cheeks. *Nowhere is safe.*

Grace emerged from the walled part of the garden, her apron pockets stuffed with a harvest of some sort, locking the gate behind her and then disappearing into the little house.

She soon returned to join Lexie, bringing with her some cool spring water in a mason jar. "I know you aren't feeling well, and I'm sorry," she said kindly. "Drink some water, and then I'll explain what I did."

Lexie scowled and shook her head. She wasn't going to consume any more of Grace's concoctions.

Grace nodded and took a drink of the water to prove it was fine. She then handed it to Lexie, who was eyeing it covetously. As Lexie sipped the water, Grace whispered to her, "I understand why you don't trust me right now. I can't have only one of them being sick from my food. I promise *you* will feel better soon. I have a plan."

Lexie wanted to trust the woman, but another spasm wracked her belly. She felt horrible as she hurried back to the outhouse, hoping it was vacant.

...

Grace watched as the slender girl rushed away.

She felt terrible. But if her plan was to work, it couldn't be obvious. It couldn't be only the Hills who got sick, and it couldn't be all of them. She knew if she wasn't careful, Christopher would execute her without hesitation. And if that happened, Lexie would be on her own again. Her survival was tantamount to the girl's freedom.

She had dosed two plates of breakfast with an unflavored laxative powder to get the ball rolling, so to speak. The moisture of the fluffy eggs easily masked the powder, and the parmesan cheese dusted on top disguised any residual powder. If two people, one of them Lexie, were ill, she could get something else into them to "nurse them back to health." If things went according to her plan, only Lexie would recover from this particular bout of gastrointestinal distress.

Her husband had told her about how they had been taught in the Army if they found themselves outnumbered, they were to separate the enemy. Then, the goal had been to pick them off quietly, individually, for as long as possible. You didn't want to arouse suspicion. The fewer threats you engaged with at one time, the better your chances would be.

Grace wasn't in the Army, but she was certainly surrounded by enemies. She took comfort in thinking of what her beloved husband would have advised.

When Lexie returned to the garden, she wordlessly picked up the jar of water sitting on a smooth-topped stump, which served Grace as a table. Lexie downed the entire thing in two swallows.

"Come with me," Grace said. "You need to lay down."

Lexie glared, mutiny in her eyes. She refused to move immediately, then finally gave in. She really did want to lay down. The hot sun beating down on her was making her feel even worse.

Grace had turned the small, screened porch on the side of her house into a delightful room. The two cozy sofas out there were comfy enough for sleeping on during a hot night and would work splendidly to isolate her patients from everyone else.

Once Lexie was established on a faded yellow floral sofa, she brought out a steaming cup. Lexie eyed it suspiciously. "It's only peppermint and chamomile," Grace informed her. "It will make you feel better, I promise. The herbs will settle your stomach and help to relieve the cramping. Do you want me to take a drink of it first?"

Lexie nodded, and Grace drank the concoction from the dainty porcelain cup. "See? It's perfectly safe."

With a sigh of resignation, Lexie took a tiny sip of tea. It tasted good–fresh and minty with a hint of something that tasted almost like apple. Before long, the cup was empty, and Lexie felt drowsy. She was worn out from all the trips to the bathroom.

She drifted off to the gentle music of wind-chimes as Grace left the screened-in porch.

...

When Luke emerged from the outhouse for the fifth time, Grace was waiting for him.

"Are you feeling unwell?" she asked, pasting a look of concern on her face. "Perhaps it's the richness of the food if you aren't used to that kind of meal."

Luke didn't deem to respond, simply glaring pointedly so Grace would take the hint and move out of the way.

Stubbornly, she ignored his hint. "Could I make you some tea? Lexie is also feeling poorly, but she's had herbal tea, and it seemed to help. If you'd come and lay down in the porch room, I can look after the two of you more easily."

"Fine," Luke replied in a peevish voice. "You'd better hope nobody else gets sick around here, old lady."

Grace ignored his tone and led him to the screened porch, waving her arm toward the vacant sofa. She went off to the kitchen to make some tea more tea.

After confirming she was alone in the room, she surreptitiously added more of the laxative powder to the boiling water. She stirred it vigorously before dropping in a tea ball filled with chamomile and mint. It was true that the chamomile and mint worked at cross-purposes with the laxative, but she'd added a potent amount of the eliminatory and was confident that Luke's bowels would continue to be in an uproar. He had to appear to be ill before he succumbed – he couldn't just die suddenly, or the suspicion would be on Grace.

She drizzled some honey into the tea and carried it out to him. "Drink up," she instructed. She gestured to the sleeping girl for added encouragement. "Lexie felt better almost immediately."

Luke blew on the tea and took a suspicious sip. It tasted good, Grace knew, and without further hesitation, he drank it down.

She returned to the kitchen with his empty cup. She passed the others in the dining room, engrossed in some card game.

She made drinks from an instant iced tea mix she had on hand. There was no ice, but the drink was sweet and refreshing nonetheless. She quietly brought them to the three. They ignored her and continued with their game, so she returned to the kitchen without a word. *Why bother making conversation when it could just trip me up,* she thought. *You can't say the wrong thing when you say nothing at all.*

Back in the kitchen, Grace got out her black mortar and pestle. The items she had harvested from the walled part of the garden needed to be processed. She pulled from her pockets a handful of glistening black berries from the thriving patch of belladonna and some stevia leaves for sweetness. She dropped them all into the bowl. Then she tossed in raspberries from her kitchen garden to add a rich berry flavor.

She mashed the herbs and berries vigorously with the mortar and pestle, then transferred them to a one-pint mason jar. She covered the herbs with vodka, then rinsed out the bowl of her mortar and pestle with a splash more of the liquor, scraping the sides with a spoon to incorporate as much of the herbal content as possible. She put that into the jar and applied a piece of masking tape to the outside.

She paused, trying to think what to write. She doubted that any of them read Latin, so on the tape, she wrote "*Solanaceae*" in her beautiful script. She put the jar on her sunniest windowsill to speed up the infusing process.

She would have preferred a bit more time to let things sit for weeks, but her situation warranted more flexibility.

She scrubbed the mortar and pestle thoroughly and then left them soaking in a mixture of bleach and water. With that project completed for the time being, Grace returned to the parlor to check on her other patient.

Grace noticed it the second she entered the room. The room where he lay seemed different. He had worsened quickly since the last time she had checked on him. Infection had taken hold.

There was a mild scent in the air that she had smelled before. It was a strange odor, foul yet sickly sweet at the same time. It was the smell of decay and impending death. A chill settled into the back of her neck, even though it was a warm day. She had never deliberately harmed a human being before and as a healer, it caused a sudden crushing wave of grief.

There was no time for it. She closed her eyes to gather herself, pushed that feeling aside, and went to check Rick's vitals.

He was clammy, covered in a sticky sweat, and burning up. As she felt his forehead, she could feel him shivering. He opened his eyes to peer at Grace. "I d-d-don't feel s-s-so good."

"I know, you poor boy," she replied kindly as she pulled down the blanket covering him to inspect his wound. "I'm worried that your gunshot wound is infected. You were exposed out in the woods for quite some time with it before you arrived here."

It was as she expected. The wound was crusted and encircled by a puffy red area. Gently, she laid her fingertips on the surrounding area and confirmed it was hot to the touch. Red streaks were beginning to appear around it. There was nothing else she needed to do except let nature take its course.

Sepsis was setting in.

Sepsis was a systemic infection that traveled from a wound into the bloodstream. The immune system attacks the infection, which leads to fever, chills, low blood pressure, rapid heartbeat, organ failure, and, eventually, death.

She'd seen it before and it was an ugly, painful way to die. Her first experience with sepsis was when she visited a young woman who had given birth in a home without clean running water. Childbed fever was generally caused when a birth attendant introduced bacteria into the womb with unwashed hands. She'd never forget the putrid yet sweet smell when she'd walked into the birthing room.

By the time Grace had been called in, the poor girl was violently ill. She begged the family to take the new mother to a hospital, but they refused. She treated her with a heavy course of fish antibiotics, sida tea, and a very uncomfortable cleansing of her womb with a powerful antibiotic mixture, staying around the clock for three days. Though it had seemed unlikely, the girl had survived. But the infection had wrought such havoc on her reproductive organs that she was unable to have more children.

Grace shook off the memory. She would do her best to ease the boy's discomfort.

She pulled the covers over the trembling young man all the way up to his chin and patted him gently. "Would you like some more laudanum for the pain?" she asked him. He didn't open his eyes but nodded. She went to the kitchen to fetch the medicine, stirring in a hefty amount of honey.

When she returned, he didn't even flinch at the bitter taste, so desperate was he for the relief from pain. Though his eyes were squeezed shut tightly, a single tear made its way down his cheek.

Grace took a deep breath at the sight of it. It *had to be done*, she reminded herself.

She picked up the basket with her needlepoint project, taking it to her rocking chair on the front porch. There, she rocked, and stitched, and waited.

The afternoon was sure to be eventful.

Chapter 7

Rage.

Christopher Hill was so furious that it blocked his vision for a moment.

When his eyesight returned, all he could see was his baby brother, pale, restless, and moaning. Ricky was in agonizing pain and Christopher was positive he wouldn't survive for even another day.

Something had to be done. If he couldn't save Ricky, he could at least take revenge. He would finish off the old woman then he'd go back to the farm where Ricky had been shot and take out every single person there. He'd kill the men first, and then he'd kill the children right in front of the women. Then, while they were still reeling in grief and horror, he would rape them. Finally he'd let them die slowly, alone with the dead bodies of their loved ones.

How dare they shoot his brother? How dare they shoot at him? Clearly, they didn't understand that he was to be respected and feared.

But they would. Oh, how they would.

...

When the door to the front porch slammed open, crashing against the cabin's exterior wall, Grace refused to jump. Sedately, she continued embroidering, finishing the intricate stitch she was working on before looking up.

Christopher had exited the cabin, and he was enraged. His handsome face was contorted with it, reddened and scowling. His eyes flashed indigo fire, and he erupted into a wordless bellow.

Grace finished her stitch and calmly put down her project. "Hello, Christopher," she greeted him courteously, taking a sip from the jam jar filled with lemonade that sat on the table beside her.

He reached out and knocked the glass out of her hands, shattering it against the rails of the porch.

"My brother is DYING!" he roared. "You said you could help him!"

"I *am* helping him. I'm relieving his pain, I removed the bullet, and I am monitoring his condition. I am doing everything I can do without a hospital," Grace informed him calmly. "He lost a lot of blood and was out in the woods with a gunshot wound to the abdomen. Did you really think he'd be fine overnight?"

"If he dies, YOU die, old lady."

Grace picked up her embroidery and began stitching. "That's your prerogative. You're the boss here."

"And why is Luke sick? Why is Lexie? Did you poison us?" Christopher demanded, further enraged that Grace didn't seem to be afraid of him.

"If I poisoned you, wouldn't everyone be sick?" Grace inquired pointedly. "I warned you at breakfast that the food was quite rich, and you should all take it slowly since it appears you hadn't eaten well in a while. Nobody chose to listen to my advice, and some people without *your* robust digestive system are suffering because of that."

He squinted, staring at her intensely like he was trying to see inside her mind. Grace flatly refused to squirm under his scrutiny. She continued to stitch. "I'll make something easier on the stomach for supper tonight. A nice pot of soup."

"I'm watching you, old woman," Christopher warned, his voice menacing. "I won't hesitate to put you down like a dog. The only reason you're still alive is that you have medical skills.

But if you don't get everyone healthy – and I mean EVERYONE – my brother won't be the only one going in the ground."

He turned on his heel and stormed away. Grace continued to stitch, the outward picture of serenity in her rocking chair.

But inside, her mind was turning feverishly. The discreet plan she was putting into action might be too slow to save Lexie and herself. Christopher was smarter than she'd given him credit for, and that underestimation could be her undoing.

What would James do? she pondered. As always, the memory of him brought a little smile to her lips. If James had been here, those people never would have gotten to her door.

But he wasn't here. It was up to her to defeat this evil family that had invaded her peaceful home. And she'd save the girl while she was at it or die trying.

...

When Lexie woke again, she felt better. She was thirsty, so incredibly parched that it felt like she hadn't had a drop to drink in days. She remembered the cartoons from her childhood that demonstrated thirst by a character dragging himself, prone, across the hot sand of the desert, hand outstretched, pleading for water.

She sat up slowly, testing how she felt. So *far, so good*, she thought as her bare feet touched the floor of the screened-in porch. Luke wasn't in the bed across from her, and she briefly wondered where he was.

Her thirst overrode her curiosity, and she made her way to the kitchen for a glass of water. She poured water from a pitcher on the counter into a glass that was a recycled canning jar. It tasted like the most refreshing water she'd ever had. She had to fight her instincts not to guzzle it all down in one fell swoop.

She wandered around the kitchen while she sipped. Jars of mysterious dried plants were everywhere. In front of a sunny window, more plants hung upside down from a curtain rod, where they'd been secured with twine. She wondered what these plants did. What had Grace had given her to make her sick? Was she trying to hurt Lexie or help her?

The girl's mind raced with possibilities. She had to accept the fact that, for now, there was no way to know what Grace was doing. But she'd be watching her from now on.

"How are you feeling, dear?"

Lexie jumped, spilling some of the water down the front of her shirt. How could such an old lady walk with such catlike stealth? Wordlessly, she turned to look at Grace. She shrugged and made a "so-so" gesture with her hand.

Grace looked around surreptitiously. In a low voice, she suggested, "You need to pretend to still be sick. It will keep Christopher away from you and make it less suspicious that Luke is still doing poorly."

Lexie frowned, thinking it over, then nodded abruptly. Anything that kept Christopher away sounded good to her.

"You really can trust me," Grace told her. "I know it's got to be hard to trust anyone, but I am on your side, sweet girl."

Lexie wondered how she could possibly trust anyone after what she had been through. She looked at the floor, unable to meet Grace's eyes. She supposed that she trusted Grace more than most people, but the woman *had* poisoned her. Had she really done it to protect Lexie from Christopher? That reasoning hadn't occurred to her.

They were interrupted when Luke walked into the kitchen. He'd clearly made another trip to the outhouse. He was pale and sweating, and he didn't look well at all.

"Would you like a cup of tea to help your bowels?" Grace inquired.

"Only if it's better than your cooking," Luke responded rudely. "I haven't been this sick from something I ate since I got bad gas station sushi before it all went haywire."

"Well, I recommended that you take it easy at breakfast. You chose to eat a great deal of rich food, and your system isn't accustomed to that. Go lay down, and I'll bring you some tea," Grace replied in her best schoolteacher-will-tolerate-no-nonsense voice. "Lexie, you can also go lay down, and I'll bring you tea as well."

Luke glared at Grace, then turned and careened unsteadily from the room, eager to lay back down. Lexie shook her head. *No, she* thought. *I want to see if she doses me again.*

Grace seemed to understand her unspoken fears. "Okay, you can stay in the kitchen until it's made, but then you need to get back in bed. You've had a difficult morning, dear."

Lexie watched Grace like a hawk. The woman took a yellow mug with a flower on it and a blue mug with stripes. She added some honey to the bottom of the mugs as she put water on to boil. She stuffed two tea-balls with herbs from the shelves beside her stove. "This is peppermint," she offered Lexie a sniff from the open jars. "And this is chamomile. The two combined help with stomach cramps and diarrhea."

As Lexie watched, Grace checked again to be sure they were alone. She took the container of powder that she'd added to the eggs and put two heaping scoops into the blue mug. Grace winked and put her fingers to her lips in the universal "shhh" gesture as she put the canister back into the cupboard. Grace poured the now-boiling water over the tea balls and filled both mugs. She stirred the contents of the blue mug vigorously.

"You take the yellow mug, dear."

Lexie took it, relieved. She didn't know for sure what that white powder was, but she'd bet her blue jeans that Luke would be making more trips to the outhouse in very short order.

She was also going to take Grace's advice and pretend to be ill. A sick day of sipping tea on a sofa and not being harassed sounded like a vacation in the Bahamas.

...

When Grace returned to the kitchen, Christopher, Beth, and Jon were at the table with a deck of cards. She felt confident they were not there to help with dinner, but, instead, were there to watch her make it.

They all but ignored her as she filled glasses with the last of the day's pitcher of lemonade and placed a beverage in front of each person.

That was fine with Grace. She could pretend to be a fly on the wall and eavesdrop to see if they gave anything away. A person could learn a lot by keeping her mouth shut and her ears open.

Grace pulled out the ingredients to make a pot of soup. A couple of sizeable jars of chicken broth she had canned. Some green beans harvested from the garden that morning. Small potatoes and onions that she had dug out a few days ago. Spices from smaller jars on the shelves. The soup wouldn't take long since the broth was already done. She used her large, green-enameled soup pot.

While she was at it, she combined other ingredients and rolled out some biscuit dough. If it had just been her, she wouldn't have heated up the house and used all that precious propane, but she had to make her food stretch, and full bellies left angry people at least a little bit more content. It also gave her a reason to be in the kitchen, eavesdropping on the card game.

As she cooked, she noticed that Beth was sitting really close to Christopher. She would place her hand on his arm as she laughed. It was evident to Grace that Beth wanted to upgrade Hill brothers to the better-looking and more powerful version, but nobody else seemed to notice. She astutely noted that Jon seemed as though he wanted to impress everyone. He was like an overeager puppy, trying to please his brother and the beautiful woman at the table. Christopher casually leaned back in his chair as though all the attention was his due.

Grace thought the dynamic was interesting, and something she might be able to use, though she wasn't immediately sure how. She hid a smile as she heard the door to the screen porch slam open and footsteps rushing toward the outhouse.

She placed the biscuits in the oven and quietly left the kitchen to check on Rick.

He was worse than he had been a few hours ago. His body was wracked with chills, and sweat glistened on his skin. The sickly-sweet smell was stronger than it had been before, and his skin had taken on an even more unpleasant pallor than it had previously.

...

Rick Hill was in and out of sleep. Everything hurt so much he wasn't sure what had even happened to him. His head hurt, he felt sick to his stomach, he was freezing, and he couldn't remember why.

He was pretty sure he was dying. He remembered that he'd had a bad feeling about the last place they hit, looking for supplies. They had a routine of killing everyone who got in their way. All he'd had to do was point and shoot and then they'd have another place to stay, more food to eat...

But something had gone terribly wrong in the last place. He remembered screams and realized that the screams had been his.

What the heck had happened? Where was he now?

Some old woman was poking at him, bringing him horrible-tasting things to drink. He felt dizzy when he drank them but then he was lost in the mists of fitful dreams. Blood was everywhere in the dreams and his brothers were smiling at him, telling him to "get some."

He had no idea how he'd gotten here. He hoped his brothers were okay. They were all he had left in this chaotic new world.

...

Rick rested fitfully, his eyes opening when Grace approached him. "Am I going to die?" he asked her between clenched teeth.

He was just a boy, Grace thought, filled with regret. *Seventeen at the oldest.*

"I don't know," she replied gently. "It's a very bad wound. Would you like some laudanum to ease the pain and help you rest?"

"Yes," Rick nodded. "I miss my mom." His eyes filled, and large tears rolled down his cheeks onto the bed. Grace couldn't watch. She was thoroughly disgusted with herself despite the necessity of her actions. She went back to the kitchen to get him a big enough dose of laudanum to ease him through the worst of the symptoms of sepsis.

"Your brother has a severe infection," she announced to the three at the table. "It doesn't look good."

The sound of his chair scraping across the tile floor as Christopher abruptly arose was startling and made Grace want to jump, but she kept her emotions in check. "I'm going to make him some laudanum with honey to help with the pain."

Christopher towered over her, his rage palpable. Jon and Beth were frozen at the table, and Grace instantly suspected both had been the targets of Christopher's unchecked anger in the past.

She stirred the pain reliever in a cup with enough honey to help him swallow the bitter medicine. Christopher snatched the vessel from her hands and stalked away to administer it himself.

Grace filled a basin with cool water and grabbed a cloth. She followed him into the sick room. "Here," she offered quietly. "Wash his face with this. It will be comforting."

There was naked grief on Christopher's face. Grace saw that despite everything evil that he was, he had the capacity to love his little brother. She left the two alone and returned to the kitchen to finish preparing dinner.

Grace had been saving people from pain, infection, and illness for decades. Every healing instinct she had urged her to make the boy on the daybed better. But she couldn't. She clamped down on her urges. Her life and Lexie's depended on getting rid of these threats.

She had never imagined that she'd use her skills this way. It was the most awful thing she had ever done in her very long life.

And she had to keep doing it.

Chapter 8

Beth was suspicious of the old lady, but then she had never really gotten along well with other women. She wondered if Grace had been making people sick, or if their luck had simply run out.

She would watch the old gal like a hawk and take special care with what she ate in the future. Luke wasn't doing well, and Beth wasn't about to join him in his decline.

Before things in the world had collapsed, Beth had met Luke Hill in a bar, a real honky-tonk kind of place that smelled of old cigarette smoke and spilled beer. She'd been struck by how handsome he was as she sipped her drink, and when he started a conversation with her, she found his streak of wild recklessness appealing. She hadn't known any other men like this, who could keep up with her appetite for cruelty, whiskey, and manipulation. She thought he was the one, so taken was she with Luke Hill.

But when Luke took her to meet his family during a holiday lunch, she met his brother Christopher and her life changed forever.

The Hills were loyal to one another, so Christopher never flirted with her or even showed that he noticed her. But she knew, deep down, from the moment their eyes met, that Christopher was the man she had been waiting for her entire life.

Not only was he incredibly good-looking, but he also had an aloof manner that belied his capacity for rage. In Beth's mind, rage was just another kind of passion, and she was instantly convinced that Christopher had that in spades.

She felt uncertain about how to proceed with him, and that was a novelty for her. Beth had been strikingly beautiful from an early age when she was the unfortunate recipient of unwanted attention from family members. Her turning point had been when she realized her looks gave her power over men. She no longer looked at what had happened to her as abuse but as her own personal training camp.

She learned how to manipulate men and wrap them around her pale, dainty finger with the long, pointed nails she regularly painted an arterial color of scarlet. She didn't just play hard to get. She *was* hard to get. And because of it, most of the men she met fell all over themselves, striving to impress her. She never felt much in the way of connection until she met Luke. In him, she recognized a kindred spirit, someone who saw the world the same way she did: people were there to be used and discarded.

But then she met Christopher and realized that he was her soulmate, a concept she'd never believed in before. He would be hers, she decided. He just didn't know it yet. Luke was now an obstacle that had to be tolerated to keep her near the one who had captured her heart.

Then, before she could develop a plan and put it into action, the lights went out, society went sideways, and all hell broke loose. Luke brought her with him to the family home, and she immediately recognized that her survival in this new world depended on this family. She'd have to go along with things and wait for her chance.

She knew that chance would come.

The longer she spent with them, the more deeply she recognized that she was on a path. She was positive that her destiny, one day, was to be with the eldest Hill brother.

No matter what it took.

Maybe the old lady had given her the opportunity she had been waiting for. All she knew was that she had bided her time long enough, and she might never again have a set of circumstances like this.

Whatever she did could be blamed on the old woman. She would weep prettily, and Christopher would comfort Beth in her time of loss. She could clearly imagine how the scene would play out.

And finally, she would have the man she deserved in a time so gloriously lawless that all the old rules that had confined her were nothing but a memory.

...

When Beth quietly entered the screen porch, Lexie was already awake. Quickly, she closed her eyes and pretended to be sleeping. The last thing she wanted was the red-haired woman's attention because that was never a good thing.

As she watched through her lashes, it seemed like Beth was sneaking in, but that was silly. Why would she try to be sly? She had every reason to be in there to check on her boyfriend. Maybe she was just being careful not to wake Luke up from his exhausted slumber.

But Lexie couldn't shake the feeling that something was off.

The bad feeling multiplied when Beth just stood there, staring silently at Luke. The stillness went on and on, and Lexie was just about to get up and visit the outhouse when Beth picked up a pillow from a cozy wicker chair.

Lexie didn't know why, but she froze, barely daring to breathe.

Beth held the pillow, her back to Lexie, and didn't move for a long time. Her shoulders were squared like she was preparing for a battle. She cast a long look around as if checking to be certain nobody could see her. Her gaze rested on Lexie for a long, uncomfortable moment.

Then, Beth gently laid the pillow on top of Luke's face. He didn't stir. She took a deep breath and began to quietly and firmly press the pillow down. Luke began to struggle, but he was in a weakened and dehydrated state...

...

Luke awakened abruptly, gasping for air. What the hell, he wondered, had that old hag done?

Then he realized that he hadn't been poisoned. Someone was trying to smother him. He couldn't breathe because a soft pillow that smelled as fresh as the outdoors was pressing down onto his face.

That little bitch Lexie?

The old hag?

Who was trying to kill him?

He flailed and struggled and managed to push the pillow down enough to see who was on top of him.

He froze in shock. It was Beth. Beautiful Beth, from whom he'd been inseparable since the night they met in a bar. Glorious Beth, his partner in crime. Beth, the Bonnie to his Clyde.

He should have realized that someone who had no mercy for anyone else could turn on him. He attempted to renew his struggle, but he'd lost valuable moments of oxygen when he saw he was being betrayed. His superior strength was waning due to his deprived lungs, and he no longer had the advantage.

As his thoughts faded, his last memory was of Beth, smiling down at him like she had countless times before, face surrounded by her glorious auburn hair. He grasped at the last vestiges of consciousness, trying to understand why she was smiling.

...

Beth pressed the pillow harder and climbed onto the couch, planting her knees firmly on Luke's chest. Her face was frozen in a grimace of determination. She was relentless.

He thrashed, and he fought, but he couldn't dislodge her as the silent battle played out. Lexie choked down her horror and stayed as still as she could. She dared not make a sound. She dared not move.

She had no idea it could take so long to commit a dreadful act like the one she was witnessing. It was made particularly horrible because this was Luke's girlfriend doing it. She was supposed to love him! What on earth would she be capable of with someone she hated? What would she do to Lexie?

A minute passed. Five. Was it actually ten minutes? An hour? It seemed like an eternity that Lexie was utterly paralyzed as she tried not to make a sound or move a muscle. She felt like she herself was being smothered, so difficult was it to catch a quiet breath and remain outwardly sedate.

It seemed like it took forever for Luke to stop fighting, and even then, Beth remained on his chest, pressing down the pillow for all she was worth. It was like she was under a spell, frozen in a horrific tableau.

Lexie's mind raced frantically. Would Beth kill her next? What could she use as a weapon? She mentally braced herself while trying to keep still and continue faking sleep. She swore to herself that sh would fight, she would scream, and she would not go down easily.

Finally, Beth removed the pillow from Luke's face. She checked the pulse in his neck, then dismounted from her place on his chest.

She replaced the pillow back on the chair where it had been. Luke's eyes were frozen open in horror. Gently, Beth closed them. Lexie thought she glimpsed a cast of blue to his face through her lashes, but she couldn't be sure if it was her diffused view or if he was actually discolored.

Beth was insane, thought Lexie wildly. *She wasn't just mean. That woman was bat-crap crazy.*

When she turned, Lexie squeezed her own eyes closed and steadied her breath, forcing her body to appear relaxed. She could feel Beth's eyes on her, studying her. The adrenaline coursed through her veins, making it nearly impossible to be still. But she knew that her life depended on pretending to be asleep, and she managed to feign peaceful rest and breathe evenly.

Beth watched the sleeping girl for a moment more.

Then, she quietly slipped from the room, a triumphant smile playing upon her full lips.

Chapter 9

Lexie remained frozen on her daybed for a long time after Beth left, cognizant that she was lying in the same room with a corpse but, at the same time, unwilling to move.

Because when she did – when this day progressed – she knew that all hell was going to break loose. However bad life had been, it was about to get even worse.

Finally, after a long time, she pushed herself up and, with her back against the wall, edged her way out of the room. Her heart banged against the cage of her chest so loudly she was certain everyone within five miles would hear it. Even though she knew Luke was dead, she dared not turn her back on his body, lest it somehow reanimate and grab her, pulling her down into some supernatural depths with him.

It felt like a journey of a thousand miles to side-step her way to the door, open it, and make her escape through it. She leaned against the wall in the corridor, gasping for the breath that had been robbed of her by panic.

Grace.

She had to find Grace.

At that thought, Lexie did run, her bare feet skimming lightly over the aged wooden floors. She raced to the front porch, hoping that Grace would be there in her rocker, peacefully stitching something.

She burst onto the porch, and Grace was exactly where she had expected her to be, looking as angelic in Lexie's eyes as the night she had first seen her.

The moment Grace saw Lexie's pale, terrified face, she knew that something was horribly wrong. She rose from her chair with an ease that belied her age, putting her arm around the girl and leading her over to a seat.

Lexie frantically shook her head "no" and pulled at Grace's arm, trying to convey the urgency she felt for Grace to accompany her back to the sunroom.

"Okay, sweet girl," Grace said, finally catching on to what Lexie wanted her to follow. "Show me what's going on."

At the sunroom door, Lexie froze. She was never going out there again. She pointed at Luke's still body, still resting where Beth had covered it lightly with a yellow paisley sheet.

Grace was bolder and entered the room to check on Luke. Before she even touched him to check for a pulse, she knew that he was gone. She had seen death many times before, and the absence of life was obvious to her even from a distance. But she had no idea how he had died. She had given him laxatives to make him appear sick so that it would be less shocking when she gave him the final dose of the poison she had prepared, but the laxatives had absolutely not been enough to have finished him off.

While she wasn't sorry that he was gone – it was one less enemy inside her home – her mind raced with the possibilities of how Christopher would respond. She had sensed a rage in him that, when ignited, could lead to any cruelty imaginable and many that had never crossed her mind.

This was bad.

She exited the room and closed the door behind her. Lexie was still waiting in the hallway, her eyes huge and dark in her narrow face.

"Come help me in the garden," she said, taking the girl by the hand. Grace felt like the garden, a place of labor to some, was the least likely place to encounter the others.

Once at the garden, she handed Lexie a pair of gloves and a hoe. "Weed," she ordered.

Lexie mutely obliged, hacking at the ground with the hoe, still visibly shell-shocked. Grace continued her monologue softly, "I don't know what happened to Luke," she said. "I didn't give him anything that could have killed him."

Lexie shook her head animatedly. Her lips moved, but no sound emerged. She wanted desperately to tell Grace what had happened but the words just wouldn't come out. She began gasping for air again, feeling the panic close in like water over her head.

"Weed," Grace reminded her. "Feel the ground under your feet. Smell the fresh, green scent of the garden. Look at the yellow blossoms on the squash plants."

After a few moments of taking in her surroundings, Grace's calming words brought her back to a place where Lexie could at least function.

"I'm going to ask you some questions, dear, because I need to know what happened. Is that okay?"

Lexie nodded, swallowing around the huge lump she felt in her throat.

"Did you see what happened?"

Another nod.

"Did someone do this to him?"

A look of distress accompanied the next nod.

"Was it you?" Grace inquired gently.

Lexie looked up from the soil quickly, shocked that Grace would think such a thing. She shook her head "no" adamantly.

"Okay, okay, I'm sorry," Grace apologized. "Was it Christopher?"

Lexie silently indicated another negative.

"Jon?"

No again.

"Oh, stars above," whispered Grace as realization dawned on her. "*Beth?*"

Lexie's eyes met hers and she slowly nodded, the horror of watching the shocking event rushing back to her.

Grace's mind raced frantically as she sought a way out. Christopher would believe it was her, and she would be hard-pressed to convince him otherwise. Was this how it would end for her?

"Lexie, you have to run," Grace whispered the order. "Christopher will kill me, and I won't be able to protect you. Run!"

Lexie shook her head stubbornly. She was not going to leave Grace behind.

"Please, Lexie!" Grace pleaded. "You can get away while they're focused on me!"

Lexie choked on unfallen tears, still shaking her head no. She would have dropped to the ground sobbing if the woman hadn't had hold of her upper arms, refusing to let her fall.

"At least go hide in the greenhouse until the worst is over. Can you do that?" Grace didn't want Lexie to watch her die.

Slowly, Lexie nodded. The tears spilled down her cheeks, sparkling in the sunlight, dampening her thick lashes. She clutched Grace's hands in her own, desperately yearning to stay there in the garden forever with the only person left in this world who wanted her to be safe. She had no idea how she'd go on after this brief respite from the hell her life had become. She didn't even want to go on.

"Promise me!" Grace demanded, leading her to the greenhouse. "Promise!"

Lexie nodded miserably, and the door closed behind Grace. She was left surrounded by the humid smell of earth and plants. She made her way to the furthest corner of the greenhouse and tucked herself into it, wishing she could disappear completely. She sobbed for the first time in she didn't remember how long – deep, wracking sobs that made her entire body convulse.

Grace, she begged the universe wordlessly. *Please don't die.*

...

Grace closed her eyes, took a deep breath, and returned to the house to find Christopher. Her mind raced, seeking a way out, trying to concoct a plan. But for once, strategy failed her. There was no way out of this. All she could do was try to keep the blame away from Lexie and perhaps commit one last desperate act.

Even though she was positive it was still there, she patted her apron pocket, where she kept her Glock. She was a very accurate shooter, according to her beloved James, and she draped herself in that knowledge like a cloak, hoping it would give her courage.

So lost in thought was she that when she heard a bellow coming from the house, she was so startled she let out a little shriek, and Grace was not a woman who was given to shrieking and hand-wringing.

It was time, she thought.

Time to face the consequences of someone else's actions.

Chapter 10

Enough was enough. Luke had spent all day in bed because he had the runs and Christopher was fed up with it. It was time for him to get up and rejoin the world, whether he liked it or not.

He stormed into the sunroom to wake up his slumbering brother and shoved him hard.

Luke's arm flopped limply off the narrow bed, but he didn't respond otherwise. Christopher shoved him again. "Get your lazy ass up!"

Luke didn't budge.

Then, the horrible truth began to dawn on him. "Luke! LUKE!" he screamed, but his brother didn't move.

And he never would.

Christopher let loose with a roar of profanities. Luke was only two years younger than him, and they'd been nearly inseparable their entire lives. He couldn't possibly be gone. What had that old hag done to his brother? Where was Lexie? Where was everyone? He was practically blind with rage and grief as he shouted his fury to the world.

He stormed out of the room, slamming open doors so hard that the knobs smashed holes into the walls they crashed against. Beth met him in the hallway, grabbing his arm. "Christopher, what's wrong? WHAT'S WRONG?"

"It's LUKE!" he raged. "Luke's gone!"

"Gone?" Beth played dumb. "Where did he go? Are you sure he's not in the outhouse?"

"He's dead! DEAD!"

"No!" Beth screamed back. She had prepared herself for the moment when she would have to portray the role of the grieving girlfriend. "I don't believe you!"

She ran down the hallway as if to check for herself, red hair streaming behind her.

A kinder man would have stopped her, but nobody had ever accused Christopher of being kind. Beth reached the dead body she had created herself, flung herself down beside him, and wept prettily, the picture of beautiful bereavement.

...

In the kitchen, Jon heard the hullabaloo and assumed that his younger brother Rick had succumbed to his injuries. He rushed out to the hallway just in time to learn that it wasn't Rick, but Luke, who had died.

Reeling in shock, he followed Beth down the hall.

Sure enough, Luke was lying there, paler than he had been in life, with a bluish tint to his face.

...

Grace froze on the path, willing herself not to flinch as Christopher strode toward her with a look of bloodlust in his eyes.

"What the hell did you do to my brother, old woman!?!" he raged.

"Nothing except give him the same tea I gave to Lexie to settle his stomach," she replied, outwardly calm.

"Then why is he DEAD?" Christopher reached her, and she felt rather than saw when his fist connected with the side of her face.

She felt a sickening sharp pain in her left wrist as she tried to catch herself before hitting the ground. Grace curled up to protect her vital organs as Christopher's booted foot kicked her again and again. *Is this how it ends?* she thought as agony strobed through her body with every blow. *I can't even get off a shot.*

"Wait! WAIT!"

A voice interrupted, but Grace couldn't tell whose voice it was. All she could do was curl herself up more tightly as pain engulfed her.

"Don't kill her! We still need her to look after Rick!" The voice of reason must be Jon, Grace thought weakly. "She's the closest thing to a doctor we're going to find! Stop it and think of Rick."

Christopher raged incoherently, but the blows stopped coming. She heard footsteps going away, but she dared not move lest she incite more violence.

Finally, after what felt like a long time, eyes tightly closed against the late afternoon sun, Grace began to mentally check herself over. First, she wiggled her toes, then her feet. They worked. Her fingers all worked. Her attempt to move her left arm sent pain rocketing through her body and made her see flashing lights behind her closed lids, but her right arm worked. Carefully, painfully, she pushed herself up to a sitting position. It hurt to inhale very deeply, it was excruciating to sit up, and she was pretty sure that at least one rib was broken, if not more.

She sat there, staring at the path she was sitting on, wondering how on earth she would stand when Lexie's bare feet appeared in her line of vision. Grace forced herself to smile lopsidedly despite the pain in her jaw from Christopher's blow. "It's okay, dear, just a few bruises," she said with fake cheer. "But I could use a hand getting up from the ground."

Lexie knelt beside her, checking her bruises and testing for spots that were painful. Then, ever so gently, she slipped her arm around Grace's waist and helped the older woman to her feet. Once Grace was upright, she did not let go and instead braced herself like a human crutch to help her inside.

Beth, Jon, and Christopher were still in the sunroom with Luke, and the two quietly made their way to the parlor, where Lexie situated Grace on the plump purple sofa. She rushed back to the kitchen for a glass of water and returned with a cloth and bowl to help clean up Grace's bruised and bloodied face.

With the gentle touch of a mother to an infant, she carefully blotted the dirt and blood with cool water and a soft cloth made from flannel. Grace leaned back against the arm of the couch, and for a moment, she allowed herself to relax and let someone take care of her.

"I believe my wrist may be broken, Lexie," Grace said. "Or at least very badly sprained. If I tell you how to do it, will you make me some medicine?"

Lexie nodded, eager to help. "In the hallway, there are some embroidery pieces on white and black fabric. Please get the one that is third from the left on white fabric and bring it to me."

When Lexie returned with the sampler that had been stitched with three plants featuring dainty dark purple flowers. Grace explained, "You need to go out to the garden and pick leaves from the comfrey plant. We'll want three big handfuls of comfrey, and you can see what it looks like from this embroidery. The white samplers are all medicinal recipes."

Lexie nodded.

"Bring it to me first to confirm it's the right plant," Grace instructed.

Lexie was relieved to have something productive to do and rushed to the garden. The plant was easy to identify, with its pretty purple bell-shaped flowers, and she had filled her basket with tender leaves in no time at all.

Once Grace confirmed she had indeed picked comfrey, she continued. "Then, in the greenhouse, look for a brown bottle labeled "arnica oil." Bring those into the kitchen and set some water to boil," Grace directed.

Lexie started the kettle on the stove before she set off to the greenhouse to fetch the arnica.

Upon her return, Grace explained how to bruise the leaves. "Don't chop them up. Leave them whole. Use the white mortar and pestle and just mash them to release the juices," she instructed. Then Lexie was to pour the hot water over them and cover the mixture with a lid. While the comfrey was soaking in the water, Lexie came back with the arnica oil Grace had made and began to gently dab it onto the woman's many emerging bruises.

"Making a poultice is simple, child," Grace told her once the water in the bowl of comfrey cooled to a tolerable point. "You're going to lay those leaves around my wrist, then soak a cloth in the tea you've created from it and wrap that around. Then you'll wrap the whole thing in a dry towel so we don't make a terrible mess."

Carefully, Lexie followed her instructions, then she covered the comfrey concoction to use the rest later. By the time she was finished, Grace was laying back and resting a little bit easier. Grace would have loved to take something strong for pain relief, but she couldn't risk being addled by the laudanum. She closed her eyes for a little nap.

Meanwhile, Lexie went to study the other pieces of embroidery in the hallway, far more interested now that she realized these were like a secret code and a magical recipe book adorning the walls.

She knew that the ones on the white background were healing recipes. What, she wondered, were the ones on a black background?

She returned to the kitchen, still pondering the ebony-clothed samplers as she began to prepare dinner from some of the jars of home-canned food in Grace's pantry.

Chapter 11

Grace leaned her head back on the sofa and listened to the comforting sound of pots and pans rattling in the kitchen as Lexie got food ready for the group.

She had always loved kitchen noises. They took her back to her childhood, when, raised by her grandmother, she would awaken in the morning to a symphony of spoons stirring, fire crackling, and dishes clanking. When young Grace had emerged each morning, her grandmother always stopped what she was doing, smiled, and gave her a hug. Then she would turn back to the kitchen and scoop out a steaming bowl of something delicious for breakfast.

A small smile played on Grace's lips as she felt embraced by the memory. She wondered what her grandmother would have done in her situation. Grace felt certain that Matilda would have taken everything in stride and effortlessly vanquished the intruders without an iota of stress.

It was a strange time in life when all your inspirations – all the people who gave you courage, unconditional love, and steady support – were gone from this world. Your only solace was to honor them by fighting with everything you had.

Now that the pain had reduced to a throbbing yet tolerable ache, she knew what she was going to do. It was a desperate ploy but the only one she could come up with in her current situation.

Slowly, she rose and steadied herself before making her way to her medical closet in the hall. There, she quickly found the sling she had sewn together a while back from a couple of sturdy bandanas. She winced as she pulled it over her head and settled her arm into it. As she gently wiggled her fingers, she decided that while the limb was injured, it likely wasn't broken. Her ribs were a different matter – they hurt every time she drew a deep breath. She dug through her stash of over-the-counter medication and shook four ibuprofen tablets out, swallowing them dry.

Then, Grace gingerly shuffled to the garden. It felt as though it was miles away instead of just across the lawn.

Once there, she pulled a big, old-fashioned iron key from her pocket. She looked around carefully before putting it into the lock of the faded violet-painted gate of the walled part of her garden. She slipped inside and closed the gate behind her.

Inside, she was greeted by her affectionate gray cat, Nightshade. The feline had wisely chosen to make himself scarce, seeming to divine that the intruders were dangerous. He rubbed against Grace's legs joyfully.

She sat down on the wooden bench inside the walled garden for a little rest as she continued plotting. Nightshade hopped up beside her, purring. She looked around her secret garden with a glow of pride. She had been collecting these specimens for decades. Every plant within it had power – to kill, to maim, and, in the right dose, to heal. She kept them behind a wall for the safety of those who might wander past, whether on two legs or four. They were unique plants collected from all over the world. Some had to be wintered in her greenhouse, and some thrived year-round in this place. She could never get enough of the smell – earthy and botanical, with a hint of what had always felt to her like some kind of ancient knowledge, nearly lost to this modern earth.

As she breathed it all in, she felt energized, like she was one with this mysterious place she had created over the years.

When she got up again, she filled her apron pocket with the driest leaves on her potted coca tree. Coca was the predecessor of cocaine and was a plant that was sacred to the ancient Incans. She treasured the plant she had gotten ahold of and had nurtured it carefully. The pot it thrived in was on wheels and spent winters in her greenhouse. To make the illegal drug required a chemical extraction of some compounds, but the leaves had other medicinal uses, making this little bush a valued part of her medicinal garden. A person could chew the leaves for energy without concern about the addictive qualities of the processed drug.

Her harvest was complete, so she slipped back through the gate and locked it securely. Then she made her way into the weedy meadow behind her property and harvested some leaves from the prickly sida plants growing wild there, careful to avoid sticking her fingers on the sharp, hairy spines on the stem. On her way back to the little cottage, she visited her greenhouse workroom, filled with jars and vials. There, she grabbed a bottle of sida tincture she had made last summer. It was a powerful natural antibiotic that would slow the progression of Rick's sepsis.

It had to at least seem like Rick was getting better if she intended to stay alive. He could chew some coca leaves to get a boost of energy and dampen his pain, and she could treat his wound with a poultice and his system with an herbal medication to hold off the sepsis for a few more days.

Grace knew that she was nearly out of time. The others had to be dealt with as quickly as possible if she and Lexie were to survive. The clock had run out on the slow approach she had initially planned.

...

When Grace entered the kitchen, the three somber intruders at the table froze and stared at her silently, eyes filled with accusations.

She ignored them and set to work as though they hadn't invaded her kitchen. She set some water to boil. Then, after grabbing the white mortar and pestle, she pushed the bowl against her abdomen to keep it steady, and, using her good hand, lightly bruised the coca leaves. She covered them with some of her precious remaining granulated sugar, scraping it all into a sweet dish decorated with a pink and yellow floral pattern.

Then she put those aside and added the prickly sida leaves she had harvested into the bowl without rinsing out the residual coca leaves. She mashed it all together with as much energy as she could muster using only one hand, then added just enough water to create a paste.

She added a splash of laudanum and a hefty dose of sida tincture to a mug, then covered it with boiling water. A copious helping of honey was added to mask the bitterness.

"Lexie?" she called out. The girl instantly appeared at her side. "Please help me carry this in to care for Rick so we can try to help with his infection."

Lexie nodded and placed the mug, bowl, and plate of sugared leaves onto an old bamboo tray to carry them into the parlor, where Rick lay, pale and feverish. Christopher's chair squeaked loudly as he shoved it back with a clatter and rose to follow them. He wasn't letting the old lady be out of his sight when she was with Ricky.

In the parlor, Grace used her good hand to smooth Rick's hair back from his hot brow. He was running a high fever, she discerned. "Please go get a cloth and a bowl of cool water, Lexie, dear," Grace ordered. Rick's lashes fluttered open. His eyes were dark with pain and she thought of her own boys with a pang of sorrow. "This is going to help you feel better, son."

"Help him to sit up," she addressed Christopher, who looked pained to be taking an order from the old woman he had determined to be the enemy. Wordlessly and with more gentleness than she had expected, he aided his brother in sitting up.

Before Grace could get the mug of laudanum and sida tincture up to Rick's mouth, Christopher demanded, "You try it first, old lady."

"Gladly," said Grace. Her arm and ribs were throbbing mightily, and though she had no need for a systemic antibiotic, it certainly wouldn't hurt her. The laudanum would provide some blessed relief. She took a deep gulp of the hot liquid, wincing slightly at the bitterness of the combined herbs.

Christopher was mollified and took the cup from her. He held it to his brother's lips and said, "Drink it down, Ricky. It'll help with the pain."

Dutifully, Rick drank down the rest of the foul-tasting brew.

Grace instructed Christopher to help Rick lay back down, and then she went to work on his wound. First, she tested the temperature of the poultice she'd made – it had cooled to a degree that wouldn't cause undue pain. She gently scooped the goopy concoction onto the wound, then laid clean gauze on top. She passed a clean bandage to Christopher. "Wrap this around his middle to keep the poultice in place."

"I don't take orders from you," he retorted. It was time to put his foot down.

"Well, if you hadn't broken my arm, I would do it myself," Grace asserted crisply. "But if it's to be done, it will have to be someone with two good hands."

Christopher glared at her but complied. Once that was done, she spoke to Rick. "I'm going to give you a leaf with sugar on it to chew. It will make your mouth feel numb, but it will help ease your pain and make you feel –"

"Wait," Christopher interrupted. "You go first."

Concealing a small smile at his suspicion, Grace took one of the leaves and chewed on it. As she'd warned Rick, the inside of her mouth felt like she'd visited the dentist and been injected with Novocaine. In fact, that was another use for the coca plant. You could chew the leaves to help manage the pain of a dental problem. It could also work as a mild topical numbing agent, which is why she had left some in the poultice.

She raised a brow in askance at Christopher and gently placed a leaf in Rick's mouth when the older brother nodded. The boy made a face but chewed it dutifully. She followed it with a couple more leaves, then rose to let him rest. She was certain her treatment would provide at least the illusion of an improvement between the pain relief, the energy boost, and the herbal antibiotic she'd dispensed in both topical and oral form.

Lexie questioningly looked at the tray, then at Grace. "Yes, let's take that back to the kitchen," Grace acknowledged her unspoken question. When the two returned to the kitchen, they were alone.

Dirty dishes had been abandoned on the table. Lexie pulled out the most comfortable-looking chair for Grace and gently pushed her toward it. Then she cleared the table and brought Grace a bowl of the soup she'd held back while the others had dined. Even though the soup was no longer piping hot, it was tasty, and together, they ate in companionable silence.

They'd require all the strength they could get if they were going to survive.

After they ate, Lexie set about washing the dishes and setting the cozy kitchen back to rights while Grace gazed out the window, watching the fireflies dance in the early darkness.

Chapter 12

Beth watched Christopher through damp lashes. The love of her life was digging a grave with his brother, Jon.

There was a seething, simmering rage in Christopher, and Beth found it strangely appealing. When he pulled off his shirt in the humid mid-summer evening, she admired his strong, lean upper body. She continued to disguise her feelings, allowing silent tears to trickle in silvery streaks down her alabaster cheeks.

Her goal was so very close.

When the hole was complete, Beth crouched beside the form of her deceased boyfriend. He had been lovingly wrapped in one of Grace's faded floral sheets by the very person who had killed him. She wept prettily at first, then began outright sobbing with faux grief, flinging herself across the corpse as though devastated by her loss. When the two men lowered Luke's body into the hole, she lay on the ground, prostrating herself and wailing inconsolably.

Christopher gently helped her to her feet, and she secretly cheered, though she was careful not to let the satisfaction show on her face. Her plan was working. Jon stayed to fill in the hole as Christopher led the seemingly bereaved beauty away from the awful sight of shovels full of earth falling onto the body in the ground.

Grace and Lexie watched the entire theater from a small window facing the back of the house. They looked at each other in disgust at Beth's dramatic manipulations.

"I can't say that they don't deserve each other," Grace mused. "But together, they'll be even more dangerous. The good news is that Christopher will probably leave you alone in favor of Beth for now."

Lexie shuddered visibly.

Grace patted her arm. "It's only a temporary solution, dear. We have to take this farm back if we want to survive. Are you with me?"

Lexie nodded solemnly. She didn't even care if she died. She was not prepared to become Christopher's plaything and Beth's slave again. She'd only known Grace for a short time. She'd been poisoned by her, for crying out loud. But Lexie was enough of a reader to know that heroes sometimes have to do unpleasant things to overcome their oppressors.

She trusted Grace.

With Lexie's nodded agreement, Grace felt more confident in her plan. She decided to watch for her opportunity.

She turned to head back to the parlor and administer more medication to make it appear that Rick was recovering...at least for now.

...

The moment Grace had been waiting for came sooner than expected.

She awakened shortly after dark had completely fallen. It took a moment before she realized what had awakened her.

From the kitchen came two angry, raised voices.

Beth and Christopher were arguing.

Loudly.

"That was my BROTHER!" Christopher shouted.

"I miss him too!" replied Beth, her voice high-pitched and seething with drama. "I was just hoping for comfort from someone who loved him."

"His body isn't even cold in the ground yet, and you're throwing yourself at me. You aren't even my type," he sneered. "Why would I want my brother's leftovers?"

Grace swore she could feel the temperature rising with Beth's rage. A slap rang out, the screen door slammed open against the wall of the house, and fleeing footsteps hurried away from the little cabin.

She wasn't quite sure who had left the house until she heard a masculine chuckle coming from the kitchen.

It looked like Beth was going to play right into Grace's hands.

Her battered body ached as she arose from the sofa where she had slept. Lexie was still curled up asleep on the chair, and Rick was on the daybed, also unaware of the argument.

Grace made her way to the front door and opened it just enough to slip through but not enough to make it squeak on its hinges. She knew the property like the back of her hand and could easily traverse it in the darkness. On this particular night, the moon was nearly full. It cast an ethereal silver light on the property.

It only took her a few moments to locate Beth in the back garden, sitting on one of the benches in the conversation area under an arbor of purple wisteria. She'd expected the younger woman to be weeping. Instead, her face was pale in the moonlight, dispassionate and cold as ice.

Her composure was even more unsettling than tears would have been.

Grace sat down on the opposite bench and probed gently, "Are you okay? Is there anything that I can do?"

Beth glared coldly in reply, still furious with Christopher. She was outraged by how he had spoken to her, stunned he didn't realize that they were soulmates, and strongly considering whether or not she even wanted him anymore. Good looks or no good looks, nobody spoke to her the way he had and got away with it.

"It was just terrible how he spoke to you. I'm sorry. It must have been very hurtful, and you don't deserve that," Grace continued, making her voice deceptively kind, gentle, and understanding.

Beth had always enjoyed praise and assessed Grace, scanning her face and demeanor for honesty.

"I only wanted him to hold me," Beth lied in a sad, small voice. "He took it the wrong way, and now I've lost Luke *and* the people I thought were my family."

Grace leaned over to pat Beth's knee in sympathy.

"Dear girl, you can't tolerate such disrespect."

"I can't, but I guess I'll have to for now. I can't get by without their help. I have no money, no weapons, nothing."

"What if I could help you with that?" Grace inquired. "If you meet me in the morning, I can take you to where I have some things hidden that you may find of value. I'll split them with you."

Beth tried to clamp down on her greed before it showed on her face. She wouldn't be splitting anything with this old crone. Still, she replied in a voice tremulous with gratitude, "You'd do that for me?"

"Of course, dear. We women must stick together, mustn't we?" Grace pretended to believe Beth was sincere.

"Thank you so much," Beth cried again, crocodile tears slipping down her cheeks. Grace had never seen anyone cry and look as pretty as Beth did. "When and where should I meet you? Can't we do this now?"

"No, we'd never be able to get there safely in the darkness," Grace bought some time. "Meet me in the vegetable garden when you get up. Wear your most comfortable shoes and bring anything you don't want to be without. But don't let Jon and Christopher see you with a backpack," she warned.

"It's a deal," Beth agreed. Inwardly, she rejoiced. She had always been incredibly lucky, and she was not at all surprised when her luck continued. While she was stunned by Christopher's rejection, leaving with this old woman's treasure would be the best revenge.

Grace smiled beatifically as she watched Beth walking gracefully through the moonlight back to the house, her coppery hair dark in the shadows of the night.

Once Beth was out of sight, her smile disappeared, and a look of grim determination replaced it. She had work to do, and with only one good arm, she'd need Lexie's help to do it.

She returned to the house and got some more ibuprofen from the closet.

Once in the parlor, she didn't slumber. She sat up straight on the sofa, her wheels turning rapidly as she filled out the details of her plan and waited for the rest of the household to fall deeply asleep.

...

When the moon had risen directly overhead, Grace gently shook Lexie awake, placing her fingers over her own mouth in the universal "shhh" symbol. Even though Lexie didn't speak, Grace wanted to be sure she wouldn't make a racket by leaping off the sofa, startled. After her time with the Hills and Beth, Lexie was quick to awaken fully. In an instant, she sat bolt upright.

"Come with me," Grace whispered close to her ear. "I need your help."

Lexie nodded. Like Grace, she carried her shoes in her hand as the two slipped out the front door. Silently, they made their way to the greenhouse, where they could speak without the risk of being overheard.

Grace outlined her plan to Lexie. "What I need is for you to carry a couple of heavy containers. I can't do it with just one arm."

Lexie nodded and put her shoes on in preparation. Grace showed her two large industrial jugs, each holding five gallons of liquid. "They're heavy. Just take them one at a time," she instructed. Before they left the greenhouse, Grace tucked a small oil can into the pocket of her apron.

Grace led the way behind the greenhouse, past the locked and gated garden. She pushed aside some brush that hid the entrance to a trail Lexie hadn't known existed. Grace piloted them up a set of steep steps carved into the earth that took them up the hill to an area that Lexie hadn't yet seen.

When they got to the top of the steps, a metal building was halfway buried into the side of the mountain. Lexie frowned, trying to figure out what the building was. Grace unlocked the door and the hinges screamed in protest. She grabbed the large flashlight that was hung on the wall beside the entrance and shone it into the container.

Lexie looked around to see that they were in a small shipping container. Inside it were dusty wooden shelving units pushed against the walls, buckets, and baskets. A small chest filled with straw was on the left side of the room, open with a few withered potatoes left. About a dozen filled Mason jars topped with grime and a couple of old dry squash were the only things on the shelves.

"This is my old root cellar, where I used to store food over the winter," Grace informed her. "Now it's harder to get up here, so I use the cellar beneath the house. Please, put that jug down by the door and help me move some things."

At Grace's direction, two of the shelving units were pulled away from the wall to create a small "room" at the very end of the container.

Lexie returned to grab the other jug from the greenhouse while Grace continued creating her trap.

She moved the empty baskets onto the shelves that had been moved to obscure what was behind them. With one arm, she dragged the chest full of straw back into the small room she had created and latched it securely. Before Lexie returned with the second jug, Grace oiled the squeaky hinges on the door to the container and was satisfied when they no longer made noise when it was swung open or closed.

When Lexie had returned, Grace propped up two 5-gallon buckets on small blocks of wood, putting each at an angle. "Be very careful not to spill any," she cautioned as she instructed Lexie to fill the buckets with the contents of the jugs she had brought up. Grace laid the bucket lids on top of them but didn't fasten them down.

Their work was done.

Grace returned the flashlight to its place, closed the door firmly, and slid home the bolt. Grace fervently prayed that her plan would work.

The women slipped through the moonlight back to the house to get a little bit of sleep before the rest of the household awoke.

Chapter 13

Grace awoke with far too little sleep to the enthusiastic morning songs of the birds. When she reluctantly opened her eyes, she saw that it was fully daylight. Stifling a groan, she sat up painfully to find that Lexie was already awake.

"Good morning, sweet girl," Grace greeted her.

Lexie gave a small smile. She still hadn't spoken a word, and Grace wasn't about to push her. They communicated just fine.

Grace said, "When I go up the trail with Beth this morning, I don't want you coming with me."

Lexie adamantly shook her head in protest, and Grace held up her hand to stop her. "Lexie, you have seen so much. Please let me spare you this. Please. Besides, it'll help cover my absence if you're making breakfast."

Lexie looked conflicted but finally, reluctantly, nodded her agreement.

When they made their way to the kitchen, Grace selected a sturdy walking cane from the stand in the hallway. She didn't actually need a cane, but it would reinforce the belief that she was old and feeble. It could also be used as a weapon if worst came to worst, but she wasn't very confident in her ability to swing it hard with just one hand. She couldn't risk the sound of a gunshot, though, so at least this would be something silent.

She could not fail.

Lexie and Grace shared a quick breakfast of jam with toast, then went their separate ways.

...

When Beth woke up, she stretched like a cat. A small smile was on her lips as she thought about how she was going to double-cross the old lady. She'd take her treasure and weapons, then kill her.

Then she'd leave and go someplace where she'd be more appreciated...more worshipped. While she wished she could go back to the house and kill everyone to get some payback, she didn't dare risk it. Even though Christopher wasn't worthy of her love anymore, her survival instincts overrode her urge for instant justice. He would be just as likely to kill her. And she knew how sadistic he was – he'd enjoy doing it.

She deserved adulation, not to be cast aside by the likes of Christopher Hill. They could have been so much together. One day, she assuaged herself, she'd find him, and she would have her revenge then.

She was confident it would happen. She had led a charmed life once she moved into her own power. Things had always gone in her favor.

Beth dressed in jeans and a t-shirt, then ran a brush through her red hair and quickly put it into a thick, glossy braid. Then, she began loading her backpack with the few possessions she'd managed to keep since the world turned upside down. She threw a blanket over her shoulders to disguise the fact she was fully dressed and carrying her pack. To anyone else, it would look as though she'd just woken up and was making a trip to the outhouse.

...

By the time Beth made her way out to the garden, Grace had been weeding for the better part of an hour. She was lost in the pleasant sensation of having her hand in the dirt when she heard footsteps behind her.

Beth fixed a soft, vulnerable look on her face, but it was impossible for her to hide the calculating coldness in her eyes. Despite Grace's warning against it, Beth had arrived with a backpack stuffed full of her belongings and had a water canteen slung around her neck. She was ready to leave, and Grace knew that they needed to make haste before they were seen.

Grace pretended she didn't see the look in Beth's eyes. Her plan depended on Beth believing she was successfully duping Grace. She looked around to be sure they weren't being watched, then picked up her cane and hobbled off after a "come with me" gesture.

Sympathetically, she said, "I just can't bear to see another woman mistreated the way you have been. We should not be taken for granted. You're too special for that nonsense."

She led Beth to the place where branches covered the path to the old root cellar. After pushing the branches out of the way, the women climbed up same path she and Lexie had traversed the night before. Once they were out of earshot of the house, she told Beth, "First,

I'm going to take you to my savings, then I'll take you to where I have some guns and ammunition stashed."

Outwardly, Beth smiled. Inwardly, she scowled to herself. It was going to take longer than she had expected to deal with this since the items were stored in different places, and she'd have to go back for the rest of the money.

"What kind of savings is it?" Beth asked casually.

"Gold and silver coins, some jewelry that I hid when things went bad. I'm going to give you part of the coins, but the jewelry is sentimental, you understand."

"Of course," Beth agreed with a false smile. "I wouldn't dream of taking your sentimental items."

Slowly, Grace picked her way up the path she had traversed hundreds of times over the years. It was essential to her plan that Beth be confident Grace was weak and infirm.

When they finally arrived at the root cellar doors, Grace leaned against the wall, acting as though she needed to catch her breath. She let Beth slide the bolt to open the shipping container. Grace reached in and got the flashlight, turning it on to illuminate the room.

"What's that smell?" asked Beth, wrinkling her nose in distaste.

"It's just some chemicals I put in to keep the rodents away." Grace fabricated the lie quickly.

Beth was a city girl, not a farm girl, and she had underestimated her opponent, so she took Grace at her word.

"I need to rest for a minute," Grace panted, leaning heavily on her cane. "The gold and silver are in the trunk behind those shelves. Unlatch it and look under the straw. It's at the very bottom. You can have half of the silver and the gold. Then we'll go get you a weapon."

Beth thought about attacking the old lady right away, but she really needed a weapon. She discarded the thought, consoling herself with the plan that the instant she got the firearm, she'd end that old woman with one to the head. She hurried to the back, intent on securing her treasure. She opened the trunk and began pawing through the straw, oblivious to anything but the precious items that awaited her.

Grace pushed over the first bucket she had propped up on a wooden block for ease, letting the bleach stream onto the floor. Then she knocked over the second one, which was filled with ammonia. The blocks they had been propped up on made the act easy, even for an older woman with just one good arm.

The odor of the combination of fluids began to fill the shipping container. Grace coughed and quickly slipped out the door before she was overcome and before Beth noticed the spills. She quietly closed the doors, glad she had oiled the noisy hinges. By the time the fumes fully reached the back of the container where Beth was, Grace had already slid the bolt home that locked the container from the outside. There, she waited.

She didn't have to wait long.

Beth began banging on the door, coughing relentlessly, pounding furiously. "Let me out, you old hag!" she raged. "You bitch! I'll kill you!"

Grace was thankful they were far enough away from the house that only she could hear Beth's cries and her fists banging on the metal walls of the building. The woman unleashed wave after wave of profanity between coughs and gasps, her voice becoming increasingly raspy. Finally, she could curse and swear no more.

It was so strange, Grace mused, to be standing in the beautiful forest, the sun streaming through the trees. The setting was like a storybook place of magic where you might catch a glimpse of dancing fairies. The birds were singing joyfully. Meanwhile, something horrifying was happening in the dark shipping container right behind her.

Finally, the coughing had ceased. It took longer than Grace had expected, and even though she had despised Beth, listening to someone die from chloramine gas would indeed haunt her for a long time to come. As every person who has cleaned a bathroom knows, when bleach and ammonia mix, they can create a toxic gas. If they mix in an enclosed space, the gas they emit can be deadly in a very short period of time. The gas killed by causing severe lung damage, edema, and cellular damage. The initial signs were difficulty breathing. Soon the person would lose their voice. Finally, their airway would close completely due to the swelling in their respiratory system. At that point, without rapid and extensive medical intervention, death soon followed.

The grim act was totally at odds with Grace's perception of herself as a healer.

But it was the only way she could save Lexie from a terrible fate. And she needed to steel herself, because she was just getting started.

When all had been quiet for a while, she cracked open the door to the storage unit, holding her breath against the onslaught of toxic chemicals. Beth's face was frozen in a silent scream and her eyes were wide open, as though in fear. Her skin looked raw and blistered, and her bulging eyes were bloodshot. She was no longer beautiful. Instead was a hideous sight that looked like something from a horror movie. Since she was certain that Beth no longer resided on this earthly plane, Grace closed the door and bolted it shut, then solemnly made her way back down the steep path and slipped into the gated garden for a few ingredients.

...

When Grace emerged, her pockets stuffed, she found that Jon was helping Rick to the outhouse. The teenager looked like he might have overestimated his capabilities in walking that far, but he appeared determined to get there.

She nodded a greeting and entered the house.

Lexie was in the hallway, studying the embroidered samplers. She looked at Grace with questions in her eyes. Grace nodded. "It's done," she whispered.

"Are you interested in herbal remedies?" asked Grace in a louder voice.

Lexie nodded.

Grace explained, "The samplers on the white backgrounds show the ingredients of different herbal remedies." She pointed to one with a rose on a long stem from which the bark was peeling, some small white flowers, purple flowering spikes, and something that resembled peppercorns. "For example, this one is for women's cramps. It contains crampbark, chasteberries, and chamomile, which are made into lovely tea. I grow all the plants for these remedies here on the property. Later I can show you if you like."

Lexie smiled widely and nodded. It was the first time Grace had seen her smile and it lit up her face and made the girl even more lovely.

She brushed past to go into the kitchen. Lexie followed closely on her heels.

Grace pulled the bottle marked "*Solanaceae*" off the shelf, then her black mortar and pestle. Smooth black berries were plucked from their stems, and she held the bowl still by pinning it between her injured arm and her stomach. As she crushed the new berries, Lexie watched with renewed interest.

"These berries are from the belladonna plant. This product is not for you to consume, understand?"

Lexie nodded in the affirmative.

Next, Grace added some raspberries from the edible garden and combined the two. "The raspberries will make it taste even sweeter," she informed the girl. Topping the bottle with a funnel, she asked Lexie to scrape the contents of the bowl into the bottle using a metal spoon.

Next, Grace filled the wide-mouthed pint jar all the way to the top with honey. It had the appearance of a fruity syrup and would taste just as sweet. "Now, we'll let it sit until we're ready to use it. Remember – do *not* consume this," she instructed sternly. The mixture needed to sit for at least one more day.

Meanwhile, she needed to make sure Rick continued to show signs of improvement. She took some sweetened coca leaves and laudanum tea with her as she went to check on his apparent progress. The sida tincture she had given him had slowed the infection enough that he would look marginally better. If she continued to provide him with that treatment, he would, in fact, recover.

But she wasn't practicing medicine these days. Grace had to use her knowledge for different purposes if she and Lexie were to survive.

...

Afterward, Lexie returned to the hallway, searching for the berries she'd just added to the bottle of syrup. She found them on a black sampler. The sampler had dark berries, purple flowers, red berries, and bees buzzing around them. Mysteriously, the words stitched on the sampler read:

Hot as a hare,

Blind as a bat,

Dry as a bone,

Red as a beet,

Mad as a hatter.

Full as a flask.

She was certain that this was what Grace had just made and that she was about to find out what the black samplers meant.

Chapter 14

When Christopher awakened, he immediately went to check on his little brother. The old lady was in the room giving him tea and those mysterious leaves again. It seemed to be working because Rick had some color in his face and his eyes were no longer clouded with pain and fever.

"How are you feeling, Ricky?" he inquired, tousling his younger brother's hair.

"Better," replied Rick. "I even went to the outhouse this morning."

Christopher nodded his approval and beamed at his brother. It appeared that letting Grace live had been the right decision, as much as he distrusted the old woman.

He followed Grace into the kitchen, where Lexie was cooking breakfast, and Jon was waiting expectantly at the table.

"Tonight, you're sleeping upstairs," Christopher warned the girl with a sinister edge to his voice. "I've had enough of you hiding out."

Lexie did not meet Grace's eyes, but she swallowed visibly. Then, she simply nodded and kept her face expressionless.

He didn't like that. He liked it better when she visibly feared him. He consoled himself that later, he would make sure that she did.

He joined Jon at the table, and Lexie wordlessly brought them their plates of steaming hot food.

Idly, Christopher wondered where Beth was. He wanted to rub his relationship with Lexie in her face. He supposed she was off pouting because he had turned her away. He tucked into a plate of scrambled eggs and toast, looking forward to a sadistic afternoon of putting Beth in her place, followed by a night with Lexie.

It was time to remind people who was in charge around here.

...

By mid-afternoon, Christopher was positively livid that Beth hadn't yet made an appearance. He had burst into the room she had shared with Luke only to find it empty, with rumpled sheets showing she'd slept there. She hadn't come down to eat, and that bitch was avoiding him.

Enough was enough.

He stomped out to the garden, where Lexie and Grace were working in companionable silence. "Where is Beth?" he demanded.

Grace stopped snipping off dead leaves from her vegetable plants and met his eyes. "I don't know. She seemed upset last night. I'm sure it was because of Luke's death," she lied calmly.

Christopher grabbed her and dug his fingers into her good arm. "If you don't want me to break this arm, you'll find her. Now." He issued the order coldly.

Grace wanted to plunge her shears into his face, but with one arm, she wasn't confident she could take him down. Her mind raced frantically, but she had no options that wouldn't bring the entire family down on her. "Have you searched the house?"

"What do you think? Obviously."

"We'll go and look for her," Grace assured him, wincing as he released her arm.

He stormed away without another word, positively vibrating with ire. How dare Beth defy him like this? Lessons were going to be learned, and she was not going to like them.

Grace and Lexie headed toward the green-house, and Grace called out Beth's name as though she really expected to find her.

...

In the safety of the greenhouse, they sat word-lessly.

"Lexie, I'm at a loss," Grace told her. "I'm so sorry that I haven't been able to protect you and set you free of them."

Lexie patted Grace's good hand and looked at her with sincerity, hoping that her eyes showed how grateful she was. She knew Grace had done everything she could. She'd suffered a beating and a bad injury trying to protect Lexie. Now, it seemed that the clock was run-ning out.

"Lexie, just run away – go so you don't have to be with that awful man again," Grace pleaded. "You're young and your life is just beginning, I beg you, sweetheart, *go*."

Stubbornly, Lexie shook her head no.

They were completely on their own. There weren't any heroes on the way. There weren't any cops or soldiers.

Nobody was coming to help them.

If she'd learned anything from Grace, it was that sometimes, against the odds, a girl had to save herself by outsmarting those who had the physical advantage.

Chapter 15

Grace found herself at a loss. She was completely unable to persuade Lexie to leave. She had to come up with a plan, but first, she had to deal with Beth's disappearance.

When she and Lexie got back to the house, Jon and Christopher were sitting in the parlor with Rick, playing cards. Rick looked better, though Grace knew the improvement was only temporary. His apparent improvement was the one thing keeping her alive. She quickly went upstairs to the room that Beth had shared with Luke, paused for a moment, then returned downstairs.

She interrupted the game, clearing her throat. "Pardon me, gentlemen."

Christopher's eyes were positively glacial as he looked up. "Well?"

"I believe Beth has run away."

Christopher erupted from his seat, his face filled with rage. "You're lying."

She refused to show fear. "I'm not lying. I checked for her things, and her backpack was gone. She's left. She's heartbroken over losing Luke, I imagine."

"I don't believe you. She wouldn't go like that, off on her own." He advanced toward Grace, towering over her. He enunciated each word chillingly.

"Where... Is... Beth?"

He grabbed her upper arms, and she winced as pain rocketed through her injured arm and her damaged ribs.

"I can make this a lot worse for you," he growled, digging his fingers in painfully. Grace knew she'd be black and blue after this.

"Beth killed Luke."

A voice Grace had never heard before interrupted Christopher's tirade.

Lexie's voice.

Instantly distracted, Christopher whirled around to face Lexie. "So you *can* talk," he said with a sinister smile. "That will make our time together much more fun for me. It's too bad the first words out of your mouth are a lie."

Lexie hadn't been able to stand there and watch Grace be battered again. Now, the words came spilling out of her as though they'd been blocked by a dam that had broken. "I saw it happen, and she thought I was asleep. She put a pillow over his face while he was sick. It took forever. She probably left because she knew you'd kill her if you found out."

"There's no way," argued Christopher, standing to tower over the girl." She wouldn't dare."

"I'm just telling you what I saw." Stubbornly, Lexie refused to take a step back and show this man any more fear.

Christopher's mental wheels were turning as he replayed everything he knew about the past two days. He was enraged to think Beth might have betrayed the family like this.

"She can't have gotten too far." Jon stepped in, hoping to defuse the tense conversation. "Let's go find her. I'll try to pick up her trail, and you can search the property yourself to see if she's hiding."

Christopher considered the suggestion. Now that he had a new target for his rage, the women in front of him were secondary. If Beth had actually dared to kill his brother, she would pay dearly. He'd make sure of it. With an abrupt nod, he strode out of the house, slamming the door behind him.

Jon, always calmer-natured than his brother, warned Lexie, "You'd better hope she confesses when we find her. You know how he gets."

Lexie nodded and watched Jon put on his boots to track Beth.

"I'll get you something to eat in case you're out there for a while," Grace bustled off to the kitchen. She quickly made a sandwich, added some fresh fruit from her garden, and filled a canteen with water. When Jon joined her in the kitchen, she handed him a bag and canteen. "There's a trail on the south side of the property, heading down the hill. If I were Beth, that's where I'd go. It's a few miles, but it leads into the nearest town."

And, she thought to herself, it was in the opposite direction of the old root cellar.

...

Jon was relieved to be out in the woods, away from everyone. He was no coward, but he'd borne the brunt of Christopher's anger before, and if he could at all, he'd prefer to avoid it.

Once he was far enough away from the cabin not to be heard, Jon began to laugh. It wasn't too often that someone got the best of his big brother, who was far too accustomed to acting like a king and treating the rest of them as peasants. He'd do his best to bring Beth back by any means necessary, but it tickled him that someone had managed to get under Christopher's skin like this.

He had fervently wished it had been Christopher who got shot instead of his little brother Ricky. Jon was sick of being treated like a boy, when he was as much of a man as Luke and Christopher. But that wasn't how things had unfolded, and for now, he had to bide his time and stay in the background. He'd always been in the background, dwarfed by both of his older brothers' good looks.

They never realized that Jon was smarter than them because they were both so arrogant.

He loved them, but he knew that he was the one who should really be leading the group. If he had been, Rick would've never been shot. He blamed Christopher and his excess brutality for the whole mess.

For now, he'd enjoy the fact that a mere woman had gotten the best of Christopher. "Jackass," he chuckled.

He'd do his job. He'd bide his time.

One day, he'd be in charge. He would be the one with women catering to him and men fearing him.

He just knew it.

...

When Christopher returned to the house, he emanated silent fury. He spoke not a word to anyone and merely sat by the window of the parlor and seethed. Lexie and Grace gave him a wide berth, with Grace pretending to nap and Lexie pretending to read. Even his adored brother Rick seemed to be afraid of making him lash out.

It was like sitting next to a volcano and feeling tremors in the earth. You knew the molten lava was building up pressure, working its way to the top. It was coming, but you had no idea when it would spill over the sides and burn you to death.

"Fix me something to eat," Christopher ordered. When Grace began to painfully rise to go to the kitchen, he stopped her. "Not you. " He inclined his head toward Lexie. "Her. I don't trust you."

Lexie, eyes downcast, quietly arose and went into the kitchen. She pulled out a large bowl and some ingredients to mix up some batter to make pancakes. When Christopher followed and sat at the table, putting his booted feet up on the chair across from him, she allowed herself a small smile as she beat the concoction vigorously.

She thought about how much she despised Christopher as she blended the batter mercilessly with an old-fashioned rotary beater. She was done being a victim. She hoped she was guessing correctly about the sampler in the hallway and the concoction Grace had made.

She endured it silently when Christopher got up and nuzzled her neck, trying not to let her revulsion show on her face. He bit her, forcing her to react, teeth nipping to leave marks as though he was branding her as his own. "I know you can talk now," he growled the warning. "So, I won't put up with this silent treatment tonight. Do you understand me?"

Lexie nodded, letting tears fill her eyes. He liked it when she was scared, so she'd give him scared.

Christopher licked the tear that trickled down her cheek and smiled in sadistic satisfaction. That was more like it. "Neither one of us will ever forget this night."

Lexie looked at the floor and nodded in agreement. No, they wouldn't forget this night, but not for the reasons he thought.

Christopher sat down at the table, awaiting the meal that Lexie was preparing.

When the pancakes were delightfully fluffy and cooked through, Lexie stacked them on a plate. She took a jar from the shelf in the kitchen – the one Grace had added honey and more berries to today – and poured it generously over the pancakes, allowing the macerated berries to top the pancakes. She topped it with a handful of fresh raspberries and a sprinkling of powdered sugar, making a lovely presentation worthy of breakfast in a fine restaurant.

She nibbled on a plain pancake and waited while Christopher dug in with gusto. Her heart was racing, the blood pounding in her ears. She made an effort to keep her hands from shaking. She mustn't give anything away. She hoped it tasted okay and that he'd clean his plate.

When Christopher asked for more, she didn't hesitate to make him another plate doused in Grace's syrup, berries, and powdered sugar.

She recalled the mysterious words stitched onto the black sampler. Did they mean anything? She felt like they had to. Grace wouldn't just stitch something so odd.

Hot as a hare,

Blind as a bat,

Dry as a bone,

Red as a beet,

Mad as a hatter.

Full as a flask.

How long would it take? she pondered. Her mind began to race. Should she leave and go to the outhouse? Would she come back and find Christopher had succumbed to the concoction? Had this all been a terrible mistake?

Her conundrum was resolved when Christopher pushed back his chair, making the wooden legs shriek across the floor. Without a word, he left, presumably to go to the outhouse.

Lexie washed the dishes with a splash of bleach and carefully put the jar of "syrup" back on the shelf. It was nearly empty – she'd used almost an entire pint. Then she returned to the parlor, where Grace awaited her anxiously.

Lexie pulled out a box of dominoes she'd seen on the shelves and laid them down for a game.

"Young man, would you like to join us?" Grace invited Rick.

"No, you go ahead. I need a nap," he replied groggily. He'd really overexerted himself that morning and wasn't feeling very well now.

Grace and Lexie each drew seven dominoes, flipped over a starter domino, and began to play. Grace had the distinct feeling that Lexie had made a rash move, but she couldn't figure out precisely what it had been.

Chapter 16

Out of the blue, Christopher felt terrible. He felt like he did that time he'd visited Death Valley on a road trip, with the high temperatures, unrelentingly light, and an arid environment that made his very skin feel dry.

He needed some water, and he'd be fine, he assured himself.

He forced himself not to stagger as he re-entered the parlor and demanded refreshment. He didn't want to let on that he was getting sick.. He couldn't show weakness.

Lexie and Grace were on their third round of dominoes when Christopher rejoined them in the parlor. He flung himself down on the sofa next to Lexie.

"Get me some water," he ordered her.

Dutifully, she got up and went to fill a glass for him.

"Why is it so damn hot in here?" he asked Grace petulantly, blinking his eyes rapidly. "Close those curtains—this room is too bright. Are you trying to kill Ricky with your little sauna in here?"

Grace got up and closed the curtains. She was beginning to have a sneaking suspicion of what Lexie had done. When the girl re-entered the room, Grace looked at her inquiringly.

Lexie's small smile was that of a cat with a fluff of yellow canary feathers sticking out of the corner of its mouth as she handed the glass to Christopher.

She returned Grace's look and winked.

...

Greedily, Christopher snatched the glass from Lexie's hands.

He took a thirsty gulp and nearly spat the drink out. It felt like razor blades slicing his throat as it went down, yet he was so unbelievably thirsty. Even with the curtains closed, the bright light was blinding him, and he had no idea how the old woman had lit the room up like this.

He leaned his head back against the couch and closed his eyes, blocking out the harsh glare for a moment so he could function. Was this a migraine, he wondered to himself. He'd never had a migraine before but he'd heard they were horrible.

He was so hot, so thirsty. His eyes hurt.

He was coming down with something. Maybe it was the virus that had sent Lexie and Luke running back and forth to the outhouse.

Luke.

His brother.

He'd loved him.

He felt the unfamiliar sensation of tears way back in his eyes but he was too dry for them to fall.

Had Beth killed Luke? He imagined the scene Lexie had described, pictured Beth's long red hair covering her face as she straddled Luke, pressing a pillow down, suffocating him. He was startled when in his imagined scene, Beth turned her face to him and smiled. As she smiled, the skin vanished from her beautiful face, and all that was left was a gruesome skull, still smiling widely.

Abruptly, he shook himself from his reverie. That made his head pound even more and he couldn't stop himself from clutching it with his hands.

He'd make her pay, he vowed. As soon as he took a quick nap. He tried again to drink some water but it was so painful it felt as though he would choke on the agony. He stopped at the first sip.

Lost in his strange daydreams, he didn't even notice when Lexie and Grace quietly exited the room.

...

"What did you give him?" Grace hissed in a whisper when they got into the kitchen.

Lexie, still not accustomed to talking, pointed to the honeyed concoction Grace had made. The jar that had held it was nearly empty. Grace accepted Lexie's actions without question.

"It probably should've sat for another day, but it seems to be working," Grace mused. "We have to figure out where to put him, so his brothers don't see what's happened. He won't be able to walk much longer, and he's too heavy for us to carry. Also, I don't really feel like digging him a hole."

Sudden inspiration struck. She knew exactly what she would do. It would be rather karmic, considering how much of his life he'd spent terrorizing other people with no repercussions.

In the meantime, Grace brought some water to boil and prepared some tea to intensify Christopher's effects.

"I suppose I can't persuade you to stay safely behind?" she asked Lexie.

As expected, Lexie firmly shook her head no.

There was something different in the girl's eyes now. She had the look of a warrior instead of a victim.

She needs to do this, Grace thought. *She needs to save herself.*

Chapter 17

An hour had passed, during which Christopher slept restlessly. His sleep was interrupted with all manner of terrifying dreams. Monsters...skulls with the skin peeled away...the ghosts of all those he had killed since the world turned upside down. The visions haunted him...terrified him...he couldn't seem to awaken from the hellish nightmare world that held him captive. He wanted to scream, but his throat and mouth were so parched he could barely get out a sound. His skin felt hot and inflamed like the worst sunburn he'd ever had.

When the old lady shook him gently, he opened his eyes just a slit to keep the thrice-damned light from blinding him.

"What?" he croaked.

"I have something for you."

The old woman's voice seemed to come from far away. She had made Rick better, so she would help him. He took a sip from the cup she held to his lips, swallowing the fruity, sweet concoction despite the pain it had caused. Even though the beverage had cooled to room temperature, it felt to him like it was still boiling, heating up his mouth and throat and coursing through his veins like thick, molten lava.

He was burning from the inside out, he thought frantically.

Dark had fallen, yet the single beeswax candle on the mantle seemed brighter than the surface of the sun. Any time he looked directly at it, he felt like he was going blind.

Grace placed a cool, damp cloth on his head. It was imperative that he wake up enough to walk with them.

When he seemed somewhat soothed, she whispered enticingly, "I know where Beth is."

Her voice sounded so sweet to his ears that he felt an unfamiliar pang of regret for what he had done to her. He couldn't remember what it was but knew he didn't deserve her kindness.

If his eyes hadn't felt bone dry, tears might have spilled out of them. As it was, he felt their unfamiliar pressure and blinked rapidly to clear his eyes.

Yet, he still couldn't see properly.

He would apologize later.

He could do better.

Be better.

As Christopher began to drift off again, Grace continued to wipe his face with cool water. "Come on," she urged softly. "Don't you want to deal with Beth? She killed your brother."

Right.

Beth was the enemy now.

Christopher struggled to sit up, but everything was painful. Lexie and Grace each took a side and helped him to his feet. He wasn't really walking but staggering along, his surroundings passing him in a blur. He couldn't clearly identify whether he was inside or outside.

Slowly, the trio made their way to a path that he hadn't known was there. "She's up here," Grace's soothing voice surrounded him. She sounded like an angel. She was helping him get his revenge. She even seemed to glow somehow as the sun went down. "Wait, I need to go to the outhouse," he said urgently in a hoarse voice.

"You can go soon," Grace promised.

As Lexie pulled some branches aside, clearing the way for him, Grace's sweet voice told him to see the light ahead. It twinkled in the trees, beckoning dimly, and seemed so very far away. The sound of the wind through the trees was haunting now, and he shuddered as he wondered if the spirits of those he had harmed were following him from his nightmares into this realm.

Grace had a drink for him in her apron pocket, in an old travel mug with a lid. Impossibly, Lexie held a luminous star in her hand.

He put one foot in front of the other. Each step was painstaking. Walking took all his concentration, and he could hear nothing but the wind screaming through the tops of the trees.

...

To Lexie, it felt as though it took forever to lead Christopher up the mountainside to the old root cellar. The lantern Lexie held lit their way as they slowly climbed up the path. By the time they arrived there, darkness had fully encompassed them.

"How did Lexie get a star in her hand?" Christopher asked, his voice filled with trepidation.

Lexie looked confused.

"He's hallucinating," Grace informed her. "It won't be long now, but the delusions will get stronger first."

Finally, they made it to the clearing outside of the old root cellar where Beth was entombed. Grace dropped down on a fallen tree, exhausted. Christopher's knees buckled without her support, and he barely caught himself with his hands before his face hit the ground. Lexie was the only one who seemed not to be tired by the climb. In fact, she seemed exhilarated.

She had her voice back.

She took the drink from Grace's apron pocket. "Just a little bit more," she urged, giving him another sip of the sweetened concoction. "Are you ready to see Beth? To pay her back for killing Luke?"

...

Christopher nodded, though he couldn't quite summon up the same level of rage he'd felt before. He was so hot. So thirsty. It was hard to see in the darkness, but the lantern on the stump by the storage unit was far too bright. It reminded him of one of those flashlights that the cops had shone in people's eyes to blind them and keep them from fighting back effectively. He held a hand up in front of his eyes in defense. He felt like he desperately needed to pee, but when he staggered behind a bush to relieve himself, nothing came out.

He couldn't think about that now. He dropped back down to the ground.

Beth.

He would make her pay. She'd killed Luke and then tried to sleep with him. He tried to summon some rage to help him power through. The audacity of that bitch.

With immense effort, he pushed himself to his feet and swayed as he tried to regain his balance. Lexie had opened the door of the root cellar while he'd been resting, and a strange smell he couldn't quite recognize emanated from it.

"Hurry! She's in here," Lexie said softly, invitingly. Christopher stumbled across the forest floor, weaving and wobbling his way to the shipping container. He put his hand on the wall beside the door and stopped to catch his breath. Lexie put the lantern inside. She wanted him to be able to see what awaited him. She handed him the toxic drink.

"It's time. Go. Get revenge. Do it for Luke."

Unsteadily, he put one foot into the container. It felt damp and sticky.

Before he could figure out what the wetness was, he felt a sharp push from behind. As he stumbled in, the door slammed shut behind him.

"What the hell?" he muttered, confused. Everything seemed to spin in slow motion, and the brightness of the lantern made it difficult to focus.

Lexie's voice came to him and sounded far, far away. "You were right, Christopher. Neither one of us will forget this night."

Why was she laughing? The laughter went on and on, mocking him. But where was it coming from?

He sat down on a crate so that he could figure things out.

And then he saw a horrific sight. It was Beth. Her face was frozen in a shriek, her skin was burned and raw looking. She was very still.

He scrambled clumsily off the crate, retreating in utter fear and revulsion.

Then, as he watched in horror, the skin melted away from her face just as it had in his dream, leaving only her grinning skull. Impossibly, she seemed to reanimate. She got up off the floor where she lay and came toward him, reaching for him with a bony hand to drag him down to hell with her.

"Beth, no!!!" he screamed, his normally baritone voice shrill with fear. "Don't you dare touch me! Back off, bitch! No!!!"

Chapter 18

Even though she'd been expecting it, Grace jumped when she heard the screams begin behind the locked door of the old root cellar. They were like the screams in a horror movie, getting ever louder and more frightened as the moments passed. Christopher began to lose his voice. He was babbling hysterically – prayers, apologies, pleas for mercy.

There would be no mercy for him.

"Is there any chance Beth is still alive?" Lexie asked.

"None," Grace replied firmly. "It's all in his head and no more than he deserves after the awful things he's done his entire life."

They sat there for another moment, listening to his delusional monologue. It was unsettling, even though they knew he had reaped what he had sown.

She and Lexie linked arms and went back down the hill. She couldn't tell if the screams were quieter because of the distance or because Christopher had lost his voice or because he had succumbed to the poison.

When they reached the bottom and pulled aside the branches to exit the path, the forest was silent except for the regular nighttime symphony of cicadas, the wind through the leaves, and the owls calling out their eternal question.

...

Lexie and Grace sat together on the parlor sofa, whispering in the glow of the single candle on the mantle.

"I'm free," Lexie whispered with a satisfied smile. "I killed him."

"Yes," Grace agreed. "How do you feel?"

"Good. Strong. I thought I'd feel guilty, but I don't."

Lexie leaned against Grace, who stroked the girl's hair soothingly. Soon, she had drifted off into a peaceful slumber.

Grace could not sleep so easily. Her mind was racing to solve the problem of the two remaining Hill brothers.

She had to finish them off before they realized that Christopher was gone. She thought about her husband. What would James have done in her shoes?

Well, that wasn't a very realistic question because the Hills and Beth would have never gotten near the house if James had been there. That line of thinking was counterproductive, though. She needed to process information as James would have done and formulate a plan.

Rick was weak, and she could give him something to make him sleep while she dealt with his brother.

Jon was the bigger threat. She had to take care of Jon, and preferably not inside her home.

Suddenly, it came to her. She knew what James would have done.

She smiled when the girl with her head in Grace's lap gave a gentle snore, and then she leaned back to get some rest, satisfied that she had a workable plan.

...

The next day, Grace began her morning routine as usual. She fed the chickens, made some breakfast for Lexie and herself, and checked to see if Jon had returned in the night while she'd been sleeping. He had not.

When she medicated Rick, she didn't give him any of the coca leaves. She didn't want him to be alert. She wanted him to be drugged and sleepy. If her plan was to work, she would need to deal with one threat at a time.

For a moment, as she watched Rick drift off into sleep, she wondered if he was actually a threat. He seemed like a much nicer person than his brothers. Could she treat him and get him well? Would he be grateful and be on her side? As a mother to sons, killing this young boy seemed far worse than the other things she had done. Dare she let him live?

No, she told herself. *Absolutely not.* As soon as he realized she and Lexie had done away with every member of his family, he'd seek revenge. It was only natural.

Lexie was curled up with a book on the big purple armchair. She looked more peaceful than Grace had ever seen her. She had clearly lost herself in the story of whichever novel she'd grabbed from Grace's shelves, and animated expressions danced across her face. She looked like a different girl than the one who had arrived in a rainstorm, drenched, silent, and afraid.

Now, it was time to deal with Jon.

Grace stationed herself on the porch swing, from which she had an excellent view of the trailhead. She practiced for a moment, resting her gun on her bad arm and holding it with the good one. Once she was convinced she could hold it steady and make her shot, she braced it between her knees to rack the slide and put a round in the chamber. Then, she laid her apron over the gun on the seat.

She began working on some embroidery, swinging gently and humming as she did. Lexie had fallen asleep while reading, and Grace expected that after all she'd been through, the girl would nap peacefully for quite some time.

Nightshade seemed to sense the safety and hopped up on the end of the swing, where a faded floral pillow awaited a feline nap. Absently, she stroked his gray ears and listened to the soothing music of his purr.

Her next conundrum was what to do with the bodies. She really wasn't up to digging a hole to bury them. She wasn't going to let them rot in her yard – this place was her haven.

When a friendly crow alit on the railing of her porch, Grace smiled.

Now she knew what James would've done. It was almost like the crow was a messenger from him.

Chapter 19

The day grew hotter as Grace waited on the front porch.

Ideally, she'd have been able to hide and ambush Jon before he reached her property. It's what James would have done. But with her injured arm, bruised ribs, and outright exhaustion from the recent ordeal, she decided that it would be smarter to maintain her post and relax on the swing.

He'd never see the threat coming until it was too late. Being underestimated was her greatest armor.

...

Jon made his way up the trail.

He'd arrived at the small town close to dusk the night before, so spent the previous night in a little grove on the edge of the forest. The next morning, he pasted a pleasant smile on his face and went around asking some questions. He had seen a few people and asked them if they'd seen his "sister," describing Beth's long red hair, He knew that anyone who'd seen her would have noticed that.

After spending the better part of the day trying to find Beth's trail, he became convinced that she had not come this way when she fled. He was aggravated that he'd pointlessly made the hike and decided to return to Grace's farm before night fell again. He knew the climb back up the mountain would take a lot longer than the walk down. He refilled his canteen at a spring and began walking up the steep trail.

...

All day long, Grace sat on the swing. Lexie brought her a sandwich at lunch and refreshed her glass of lemonade throughout the day. Each time, Grace kindly shooed the girl back inside. Lexie didn't need to see further death.

In the early afternoon, she assigned Lexie to the task of keeping Rick company with a game of cards. She was to stick with the story that both Christopher and Jon were out searching for Beth.

A bit later, she explained to Lexie how to give Rick a strong dose of laudanum so he'd sleep through the night. Afterward, she could hear Lexie's footsteps, pacing back and forth down the pine-floored hallway.

Grace was on edge. She'd waited all day to put her plan into motion, and now she wasn't sure if Jon was going to make it back. The sun was dwindling behind the trees, and dusk began to fall. She wondered whether she should call it a night when she heard rustling on the trail. Was it a forest creature, or was it Jon?

She didn't have to wait long until he appeared.

By the time Jon had reached the trailhead, he was downright annoyed. He'd been swatting mosquitoes for the better part of an hour, his legs were tired, and he was out of breath from the steep climb.

He was beginning to wonder if Grace had sent him on a wild goose chase.

When he emerged from the trail, even though it was approaching sunset, he saw the old lady sitting on the porch. Initially, it seemed like she froze, but then she smiled and waved, as if she was welcoming him back.

She said something, but he couldn't understand her from the distance. She repeated it but seemed to be mumbling. This was also annoying and wasn't improving his mood. He stalked up to the porch, bristling with irritation. She remained on the swing, mumbling.

"I can't hear you –" he began. Then he froze.

...

Grace sat there quietly on her porch swing. With no lights on, she figured that she would hardly be noticeable from the distance she was from the trailhead.

She was wrong.

He did see her.

When she realized that he'd seen her, Grace gave a friendly wave and smiled in greeting. Jon waved back. It seemed to take forever for him to stride toward the house.

Grace spoke softly, drawing him in. "Did you have any luck? Did you find Beth? I bet you're hungry. We have a lovely surprise waiting for you."

Her voice was so quiet that Jon strained to hear her. "What did you say?" he yelled.

Grace spoke even more softly and repeated what she'd just said, looking down at her lap so Jon couldn't read her lips. *Just a little bit closer,* she thought.

As Jon approached, looking annoyed that she wouldn't speak up, she slipped her hand onto the butt of her Glock. She'd already chambered a round, and it was ready to go.

Just a few more steps.

"I can't hear what you −−" Jon began, then stopped in horror as he found himself looking down the barrel of Grace's gun. "Wait! My brother will kill you! Wait −"

His plea was cut off as his face disappeared into a haze of red mist. Without an iota of hesitation, Grace had shot him. Her ears rang from the gunshot, and she hoped Rick hadn't awakened. She couldn't hear Lexie's footsteps in the hall anymore from the ringing in her ears and was surprised when she appeared beside Grace, looking frantic and yelling something.

"I can't hear you," Grace shouted back. "The gunshot made my ears ring."

"I thought someone shot you," Lexie cried, throwing her arms around Grace's neck.

They stood there together, embracing, looking at the gory sight of Jon's body, completely face-less.

It could have been anyone. It could have been a creature from a nightmare.

Finally, Grace broke the silence.

"Please go get the wheelbarrow, dear girl."

Wide-eyed, Lexie nodded and raced off to do as Grace had instructed.

Grace's wheelbarrow was ancient but sturdy. She'd never been able to bring herself to get one of the flimsy new plastic ones. Hers was heavier, it was true, but it could also withstand a lot more weight, something she was glad of in her current circumstances.

Together, Grace and Lexie rolled the corpse closer to the porch. She propped the wheelbarrow up on the bottom step to hold it still, and then they pushed Jon's body into it. With Grace having the use of only one arm, it was a struggle, but they finally maneuvered him into the tray, leaving a trail of gore in the grass.

It was a grim job, but it had to be done. Frustratingly, it was far more difficult than Grace had imagined. After Jon's limp, heavy body had twice rolled out of the wheelbarrow when they tried to move it, she sent Lexie for some bungee cords in the workshop.

Necessity is the mother of invention, she thought hysterically, holding back a nervous giggle.

Lexie returned, cords in hand. Finally, they got the faceless corpse secured and the wheelbarrow was ready to push. By this time, dusk had fully fallen in the forest, but there was still enough light to reach their destination.

Grace directed Lexie to the large meadow north of the cabin, where she'd harvested sida for the herbal antibiotic. Grace used her good arm to help Lexie push the wheelbarrow. Slowly, they made their way across the meadow with their heavy load all the way to where the forest started again.

Grace unfastened the bungee cords. Lexie looked at her, questions in her eyes.

"We're going to let Mother Nature handle this for us," Grace informed her. "We can't do this with Christopher's body or Beth's because they'd be toxic to the animals. We'll just seal up that root cellar as their tomb."

James had told her of something called a Tibetan sky burial that he'd encountered during his travels. In many parts of Tibet, Nepal, Mongolia, and India, the ground was too rocky to dig up a resting place. Instead, in the practice of Vajrayana Buddhism, which was the most common religion of the area, corpses were taken to an isolated mountaintop in the wilderness and left as a generous offering to scavengers and carrion birds.

Far less ceremoniously and reverently than the Buddhists, they dumped Jon's body out of the wheelbarrow and onto the ground. Grace imagined that it wouldn't take long before the forest's scavengers located their feast.

Lexie took hold of the lightened wheelbarrow, and they made their way back to the cabin without a second glance back. Once in the yard, they took turns pumping water so the other could wash up after their grisly excursion. They would deal with the gore near the front steps tomorrow during the daylight.

In the distance, Grace heard the call of a crow. The carrion birds had found the gift in the meadow.

Chapter 20

The next morning, Lexie slept in.

It was the first time in glorious ages that Lexie had felt free to sleep. The first time since she'd been In Hell that she wasn't listening while she slept, or waiting to be assaulted.

When Grace awakened, she saw that Lexie was still sound asleep. She got up and decided to revisit her regular pre-Hill-brother morning routine. She released the chickens to let them free range. She gathered some eggs from the henhouse and some fruit from the berry bushes in her garden. She put some jam on a piece of bread and ate it with a bowl of fresh raspberries. She savored that breakfast more than she had thought possible, sitting at her kitchen table, looking out the window at the gloriously blue summer sky. Soon, she'd select a book to read and sit outside, breathing in the damp green scents of the season.

However, she still had one more grievous act to commit. Although she thought that Rick might be salvageable as a human being, the risk of him seeking revenge for the deaths of his family members was far too great. She decided that she would make it as quick, peaceful, and painless as she could. He'd never even know what was coming.

She indulged in some tears as she thought about what she'd have to do. As a mother, this would be the most difficult act she had committed. Tears slipped down her cheeks as she mourned the fact that she had used her gifts to harm instead of heal. However, she had always been the kind of woman to do what must be done, no matter how unpleasant. She would wait until everyone awakened and then take care of this final task.

She lost herself in a mystery novel for hours, rocking on the porch. When Lexie finally awakened, the sun had passed its midpoint, and it was early afternoon.

...

Lexie stretched luxuriously when she awakened, and then she lay there, listening to the birds. It had been so long since she had felt this relaxed. The feeling was no longer familiar, but she savored it.

It wasn't long before her sense of well-being was replaced with dread. What if Grace wanted her to leave? What if she was angry about all the bad things that had happened at her home? Where would she go? What would she do? After this brief period of feeling loved and protected, she was bereft at the very idea of losing Grace.

She went to the outhouse, reveling in the carefree feeling of the warm sun on her skin, and then joined Grace, solemnly perching on the porch swing.

"Good morning, sweet girl," Grace greeted her warmly.

Lexie's eyes filled with tears. She had dammed them up for so long that now they burst from her like a rampaging river, uncontrollable and torrential.

Grace joined her on the swing and took the girl in her arms, soothingly patting her on the back. She didn't tell her to stop crying but instead bore unjudging witness to her grief and pain. She pushed the swing with her feet, rocking Lexie and letting her cry it all out.

When the river of tears had subsided to a few sniffles, Grace pulled a hanky out of her pocket and handed it to the girl. Lexie took it gratefully and blew her reddened nose like a trumpet.

"Do you have any family left, Lexie?" Grace inquired gently.

Miserably, the girl shook her head in the negative.

"Well, you do now, my girl," Grace assured her. "You can stay here with me as long as you want, and we will keep each other company."

Beyond words, Lexie hugged Grace so hard that her injured ribs protested. But she endured the squeeze and hugged Lexie right back.

"We do have one more thing to take care of," Grace said.

"Rick."

"Yes."

"Do you have a plan?" Lexie inquired.

"I do. I hate to do this because he seems like a nice enough young man. But I'm too worried he will seek vengeance for his family," Grace mused.

"He's not as bad as the others," said Lexie earnestly. "But he still participated in the raids on other people's homes. He still hurt people and took their things."

Knowing that Rick had not been an innocent bystander helped to assuage Grace's guilt.

She was ready to finish taking back her home. Then she'd remove every trace of the interlopers. To remove all evidence of their presence would make it almost like they'd never existed.

And it was what they deserved.

Chapter 21

Finally, Rick awakened enough to realize his mouth was dry and his eyes felt gritty. When he tried to move, pain enveloped his body and he couldn't stifle a groan.

As if he'd magically summoned her, Grace appeared beside him with her ever-present spoon full of laudanum. He was starting to not even mind the bitter taste because he knew he'd soon be drifting in a dreamscape, largely free of the pain that ripped at him right now.

"Let's get you up for a walk to the outhouse." The old woman's voice seemed to be coming from far away.

"I don't need to," Rick argued weakly.

"You must," Grace replied firmly.

He struggled to sit up. She aided him, careful not to make it more painful than it needed to be. The room swam around him, and he closed his eyes and leaned back, fighting a wave of nausea.

Finally, he made it to his feet, wobbling unsteadily. Grace shoved a walking stick in his hand for him to lean on. Once he'd gotten his balance, he shuffled toward the back door.

He had to sit on a stair for a moment after walking down the steps off the back porch. He gathered up his energy and stood, with Grace assisting by tugging him to his feet. She was pretty strong for an old lady, Rick thought idly.

"Where are my brothers?" he inquired as he stood for a moment, letting the dizziness recede.

"Don't you remember? They went out looking for Beth yesterday," Grace expertly dodged the question. "Do you need help walking to the outhouse, or is the stick enough?"

"I don't need help," Rick said manfully. "I can walk."

"It's a beautiful day, isn't it?" Grace hoped he'd look around and see the beauty.

"It is," agreed Rick absently, concentrating on putting one foot in front of the other.

Grace walked behind him on the path to the outhouse. When they were out of view of the house, she pulled out her Glock from her apron pocket and shot him in the back of the head while he admired the contrast of the deep azure sky against the vivid green of the trees.

"I'm sorry," she apologized as his body crumpled to the ground.

Chapter 22

This time, Grace and Lexie knew what they were doing. It also helped that Rick was far lighter than his brother because he was young and had scarcely been eating since his injury. Loading his corpse into the wheelbarrow and strapping it in with bungee cords was much easier, as was pushing him all the way across the meadow to the edge of the forest to make another offering to the woodland scavengers.

Lexie averted her eyes from Jon's remains, but Grace didn't. She peered at him to confirm that yes, indeed, her plan for getting rid of these bodies was working as efficiently as she had hoped. It was.

After tipping Rick's frail body out of the conveyance, Grace and Lexie made their way back across the grassy field to the edge of the yard.

As they ambled slowly toward the greenhouse, Lexie pushed the wheelbarrow. The sky began to darken suddenly. With a long, low rumble of thunder, the clouds let loose with a cool, heavy, cleansing rain.

Lexie set down the wheelbarrow and began to spin as the raindrops trickled down her face. She danced to music that only she could hear, and the rain washed away the blood on her hands and some of the grief and trauma in her heart.

She had been through the worst thing she could have ever imagined, but she had survived. She had Grace now. She had a home. She was alive. She would be safe. Nothing else mattered.

The rain became torrential and washed away the gore and the last signs that two of the Hill brothers had expired in Grace's yard. While Lexie stayed outside in the cleansing rain, Grace went in to strip the beds. She brought the sheets out, and Lexie helped her hang them on the clothesline. The rainfall quickly saturated the linens, removing the scent of the intruders.

Arm in arm, Lexie and Grace went back into the house. Grace filled buckets with freshly scented cleaners she had made herself, and together, she and Lexie scrubbed away every last trace of Beth and the Hills.

The little house that Grace loved so was no longer infected with evil and danger. It was fresh and clean. It was a new beginning. Grace and Lexie were a family now, and this was their home.

Grace thought of James as she made up the second bedroom for Lexie, spreading a lovely, embroidered yellow floral quilt over the bed and fluffing pillows trimmed with handmade lace. They had always wanted a daughter to complete their family but had been blessed with two wonderful sons instead. James would have adored Lexie, she thought. The girl was clever, loved to read, and she was a survivor.

In fact, she reminded Grace of herself when she was young. And now, she'd be raised by a grandmother figure, just as Grace had been raised by Matilda. She would share her secrets and her skills with Lexie to prepare her for the world ahead of her, just as she had been prepared.

Grace no longer felt like she had been forgotten, with nothing left to live for.

They'd saved each other.

Families do that.

Epilogue

A year after Grace and Lexie had joined forces, the two sat on the porch, enjoying the breezes of an unsullied summer.

Lexie was stitching her own sampler. Grace had taught her how to record herbal recipes in the stitches, and she was making one for a lovely blend of herbal soap she had created. She frowned over a difficult stitch, biting her lip, determined to make this worthy of hanging in the hallway. Nightshade curled up beside her, purring so loudly that even Grace's old ears could hear him. The feline had quickly adopted Lexie just as enthusiastically as Grace had.

It had been a year of healing for them both. Lexie was now seventeen. She was strong, healthy, and self-assured. She was a sponge, reading every book and learning everything Grace was willing to teach her. Her brown eyes no longer looked haunted. Instead they sparkled golden with mischief. A quick smile revealed dancing dimples in her cheeks, and she laughed loudly and often as she recovered from her ordeal.

Since there were no schools, Grace took it upon herself to educate the girl. She instructed her in Latin, herbalism, biology, anatomy, and botany, all subjects in which she was greatly well-versed. She taught Lexie about the farm and how to care for the plants and the chickens.

They spent evenings playing games and reading aloud to one another. They enjoyed indulging in crafts, making delicious food, preserving their harvests, and creating herbal concoctions.

They never discussed how Lexie had arrived on Grace's doorstep. They had an unspoken agreement to leave it all in the past.

On this particular night, it looked like rain. They'd always loved the rain since it had brought them together and washed away the taint of evil that had briefly resided at Grace's home.

And then Grace saw it.

Two figures at the edge of the woods, about to emerge from the trailhead.

She got Lexie's attention and subtly nodded toward them. The girl tensed up and put her hand on the knife that was always strapped to her thigh. Grace tried to be discreet as she racked the slide of her faithful Glock, putting a round in the chamber.

Grace's heart began to pound. "Please, no," she prayed silently. "Please, not again."

As the figures got a little bit closer, their features became clearer. Could it possibly be...

"Mom?" The figures stopped. "Mom!"

She couldn't believe her eyes and ears. Joy leapt in her heart and she ran down the steps like she was a young woman again.

Her sons, James and William, laughed loudly as they embraced her, with William picking her up and swinging her around with glee. "How did you get here?" she asked them incredulously, tears of joy streaming down her face.

"We walked," Will told her. "Jim made it down from Canada to me, then we walked here. We'd been in touch with our ham radios, so I waited for him."

"We were so worried about you!" Jim told her. "I'm so thankful you're okay!"

"I knew you'd be fine," said Will, rolling his eyes. "It would take more than an economic apocalypse to bring down *my* mom. And boy, do we have some stories for you about our long walk home."

"Darlings, there's someone I want you to meet," Grace said, still reeling with the fact that her sons were alive, well, and back home. "This is Lexie. She lives here with me."

Lexie had witnessed the entire interaction from the front porch. She was frozen in trepidation, even after she realized that these people were not unknown to Grace. Would she still be wanted and needed now that Grace's real family was here?

Will spoke first. "I always wanted a little sister."

"It's nice to meet you," echoed Jim with a warm smile.

Lexie let out a breath she didn't realize she'd been holding with a whoosh. After she had been taken, all she ever thought about was survival. She'd spent a year with Grace, learning, loving, and being loved.

And now, it seemed, she had a whole family.

"It's nice to meet you, too," she replied. "I always wanted a big brother."

"Well, now you have two!" Jim whooped, always the most enthusiastic of young men.

Together, they went inside the little cabin in the woods, where Grace would make them a lovely dinner and hear all about their adventures on the road.

The only thing missing was her beloved James. Then she glanced out the window to see a crow perched briefly on the banister, looking back at her through bright black button eyes.

She smiled. Her home was complete. Life was good.

About Daisy

Daisy Luther is a well-traveled, coffee-swigging blogger and author who lives in urban North Carolina. She is the founder and publisher of TheOrganicPrepper.com, a popular blog. Daisy is the best-selling author of 17 non-fiction books.

The Widow in the Woods is her first fictional novel.